MW00817870

AN ARTISTRY PUBLISHING BOOK
DANE, First Edition: 2018
Copyright © 2018 by A.C. Arthur
All rights reserved.
Cover Art Design © 2018 by Croco Designs

All rights reserved. This book is protected under the copyright laws of the
United States of America. No part of this publication may be reproduced,
stored in a retrieval system, or transmitted in any form or by any means—
electronic, mechanical, photocopying, recording or otherwise—without the prior
written permission of the publisher.

This book is a work of fiction. Characters, names, locations, events and incidents
(in either a contemporary and/or historical setting) are products of the author's
imagination and are being used in an imaginative manner as a part of this work
of fiction. Any resemblance to actual events, locations, settings or persons, living
or dead, is entirely coincidental.

www.acarthur.net

DANE

THE DONOVAN DYNASTY, BOOK 1

Dane Donovan is in Paris, but he is not starting over. Neither is he looking back. He's picking up where he left off and now, more than ever, is determined to get it right. Four years ago she was a mistake, so running into Zera at the place where they first met now, cannot be good. Unfortunately for Dane, walking away may not be an option this time around.

To bring her cousin home, Zera Kennedy would give up everything she worked for…including the first man to capture her heart. But now that the kidnapper's trail has gone cold, Zera is not sure she'll be able to achieve her goal, and until she does, returning to her home in Kenya is not an option. Neither is staying away from Dane Donovan once he walks back into her life.

But the moment they both let down their guard and believe in the love that gives them a new look on life, fear invades their tender reunion and threatens every kiss, every moan, every… breath they take.

DEAR READER,

We're taking the next step! Leaping forward to a new segment in the world of our beloved Donovans.

I want to take this moment to thank you from the bottom of my heart, for sticking with me and this series for so long. It is because of you and your love of the Donovan family, that I am able to open the door to a new day in their lives.

Dane Donovan was first introduced in EMBRACED BY A DONOVAN. He was the Secret Son featured in the last five books of the Donovan Series. And now, Dane has his own story. I originally had a different title for this book, but after thinking about all that this story would encompass, I knew the title had to speak for itself. This book is about Dane—the man, the lover, the first chapter of THE DONOVAN DYNASTY.

It is my hope that you will enjoy this journey Dane is about to take and that you will also fall in love with Zera Kennedy, the woman who stole Dane's heart, not once, but twice and ultimately, forever.

Happy Reading,
AC

PART I

Love, like rain, does not choose the grass on which it falls.
—*South African Proverb*

CHAPTER 1

Paris, France

"He's dead," she said, her tone void of any emotion, eyes focused intently on him.

"Just in case you're wondering what I'm doing at the museum alone on a balmy summer evening. There's your answer. Emmet is dead."

Dane did not respond. He could only stand frozen to that spot, staring.

He hadn't anticipated seeing her. In fact, he'd tried desperately to keep any thought of her out of his mind as he'd instructed his assistant to make arrangements for this trip. If he had assumed he would see her, surely he would have thought of something casual to say to her. Or perhaps it would not have been casual at all, considering the events that had taken place the last time he'd seen her. At this moment, he was caught off guard. And he didn't like it.

Zera Kennedy stood just a few feet from him and Dane

could not speak. It had been four years since he'd last seen her. Four years since she'd looked him in the eye and confirmed with her silence that the passionate nights they'd shared for two months had meant nothing, and that her heart was promised to another. To Dane's college friend, Emmet Parks.

Dane wouldn't pronounce that she'd broken his heart. He never gave his heart to be broken. Shock and disappointment more appropriately described his feelings when he'd seen Zera standing beside Emmet. He wasn't sure how he felt about seeing her now.

She looked amazing. Just as she had the first day he'd met her, ironically, right here where they presently stood just inside the pyramid entrance to The Louvre. Her hair hung long and straight past her shoulders, her almond-colored eyes assessing him. Dane hadn't forgotten the soft touch of her lips, the smoothness of her skin or its deep sepia, reddish-brown tone. And while he used every bit of restraint he possessed to keep his gaze above the shoulders, he recalled with great clarity every enticing inch of her svelte body.

"Are we going to stand here and stare at each other as if we have no words?" she asked.

Dane smoothed a hand over his low-trimmed beard and replied, "No."

He breathed in easily, releasing the breath slowly and resigned himself to the unexpected reunion.

"It's good seeing you again, Zera."

It was, he thought, even though his body hadn't quite caught up to the practiced calm of his brain. He was reacting to her in the same way he had four years ago. His fingers tingled with the urge to touch her and his blood pulsated hot and quick through his veins at the possibility of her naked body against his. He swallowed hard and continued to stare into her eyes. Zera was tall, six feet exactly, he recalled. So they were just about eye level with his six foot four-inch stature.

She nodded and her hair fell like ebony sheets around her face. Dane wanted to reach out and touch the silken strands or to tuck them behind her ear the way he used to. He refrained.

"Are you here to see a particular exhibit?" he asked.

"I'm here to see everything," she replied.

She'd said that the day they'd met. It had been raining. The sky and the landscape surrounding it a dusky gray tone with the cool drizzle of rain falling just like an old film still of Paris. Dane had run into the building, shaking water from his jacket as he'd waited to purchase his ticket. He'd only walked a few feet past the ticket booth before seeing her at the information desk where maps of the museum in different languages could be obtained. He'd tried not to stare that day and attempted to not appear as awestruck by her presence as he'd felt. He had selected the English map and noticed that she'd picked up the one in French. At the time, his French speaking skills had been rusty at best, but he'd managed to say something. And she'd smiled before chuckling. *I'm here to see everything*, she'd said to him in perfect English. *You should see everything as well.*

And he had, with her by his side. Tonight, that first meeting didn't seem like too long ago. Especially now that she was once again staring back at him, waiting for his response.

"I'm here to see that too," Dane said after the pause. "We can see everything together."

It was an invitation. One he wasn't totally sure why he'd extended.

She pushed her hair back from her face and squared her shoulders. "Yes. We can."

Now, it was too late to take it back.

Dane walked toward the information desk with her beside him. He didn't think about their past. This time he thought about the last nine months of his life. About finalizing the last details of his mother and sister's estates. He thought about having to bury the only two people in this world that he'd ever loved unconditionally. And then he thought about what those two people had done to so many others. That's why he was here in Paris now. Because those thoughts had weighed him down for far too long and he'd needed to find some peace and some calm in order to continue. When Zera touched him, snapping him out of the dark memories, he wondered if peace and calm would ever be possible.

It was a gentle hand to his arm, casual and light. Nothing for him to read into. Still, every part of him halted as he looked over to her.

"We do not need a map," she said. "I have been here so much I know my way around pretty well."

Had she come here after he'd gone? Of course she had, why wouldn't she? Besides, the answer to that was obvious since she was here now and had no idea that he would be too.

"Then I'll follow your lead," Dane told her.

He wasn't used to following anyone, in any respect. He'd made his fortune through a strategic investment which gave him the capital to buy a fledgling energy company. And in the last ten years he'd worked hard to grow that small company into Imagine Energy Corporation, a global conglomerate with ventures including oil and gas exploration and production, petroleum refining and chemical production, and the marketing of petroleum and chemical products. Through Imagine's core, wholly owned subsidiaries, joint ventures and its global affiliates, Dane employed 400,000 people. He was a self-made success, without the prestige of the family name he carried, and a forty-one year-old man who had taken care of himself since he was seventeen years' old. But he would happily follow Zera Kennedy, again.

"We will head toward the Pavilion des Sessions," she said and walked them through the riverside Grande Galerie.

Dane remembered this impressive palace and art museum, outside of it being the place where he'd met Zera. Intricately detailed murals lined the ceilings while heavy gold molding supported the structure. Along both sides, the walls held massive portraits depicting the French history.

"Toward the Arts of Africa," he said recalling her favorite location in this museum.

The look she gave him said she was shocked that he remembered. The warmth that spread through him when she smiled, said there was nothing about her he was likely to ever forget.

Zera was from Nairobi, Kenya. Her mother was a nurse in Nairobi. She was an only child and had attended college in the States before moving to Paris. That, to Dane's chagrin, was all he actually knew about her. Other than the physical knowledge that he'd accumulated during the sixty days and fifty-nine nights in her arms.

"We are going to see all of the non-European art. Then, if there is time, we will see more," she told him.

They would have time, he thought as they continued to walk. He could make the time. True, he had come to Paris with the hope of finding some balance in his life. But surely he could make a detour. Wasn't that what Zera was? Then and now? A detour from Dane's real life. Or was he getting too old for detours?

"Come on," she said and reached out to take his hand. "You are walking too slow. The museum will close in two hours."

Before Dane could respond she'd laced her fingers through his and was heading down the stairs in a quick trot. He easily kept up with her while marveling at how warm her hand felt in his. How her fingers clasped easily with his own and how much he'd missed such a simple, yet enticing contact with a woman.

Not just any woman, Dane realized when they'd cleared the steps and she released his hand. This woman—Zera. Not only had he never forgotten her, but he apparently hadn't gotten over her either. He wondered what that meant and if perhaps coming to Paris had been a colossal mistake.

Shit.

Zera was messing this up.

Being too friendly, acting too much like nothing had happened.

When so much had.

Emmet was dead.

And Hiari was still missing.

Yet, here she was standing next to Dane Donovan wishing like hell for him to touch her. Take her hand. Put his arm around her. Kiss her temple the way he'd done before. She'd wanted him fiercely four years ago. She'd allowed herself to believe in the possibility of a future with this man. A future with someone who made her laugh and aroused her in a way she'd never experienced before, or since.

But she'd given it up. She'd let that dream, the possibilities and the hope slip through her fingers.

Now, Zera clenched her fingers together, hating that she'd lost so much more than Dane in the years since he'd left Paris. She'd lost so much that in the six months since Emmet's death, she'd begun to feel desolate and displaced. Tonight, however, she'd felt inspired and so she'd left her apartment after she wasn't sure how long and came here. It was as if some part of her had known he would be here. Of course that was foolish. But Zera could not deny the spike of happy that had soared through her the moment she'd seen him. That feeling had been so foreign to her lately, she'd almost forgotten how it felt.

"You favor the terracotta sculptures," she said when it felt as if they'd been silent for too long.

That was a contradiction to the fact that she was certain she was talking too much, but she couldn't help it. She hadn't talked to anyone about art or food or the time of day to be exact, in far too long.

"That one is from Nigeria," she continued. "Conical heads, short tubular bodies and simplified faces are prevalent in the Nok sculpture. Traditional or tribal African sculptures often deal primarily with the human form. Animals and mythical creatures are also favored forms of art expression."

He did not look at her but he did nod as she spoke. His attention stayed focused on the sculpture. Zera tried to keep further comments to herself as she realized he was really studying the art work. But there was so much more she wanted to say.

She wanted to ask Dane how he'd been. How was work? Zera knew that Dane ran his own company and several subsidiaries of such. She'd also read somewhere that he'd bought shares into Donovan Oilwell, a U.S. based company with a London office. There'd also been some talk about the Donovan family and a couple of murders in the past year. But that was none of her business. Dane was no longer her business. That's what she'd said as she ordered herself not to keep tabs on him any longer. Her resolve had been working, until now.

"I have a home in New York. I've been looking for others."

Realizing quickly that he was speaking to her, Zera readily replied, "These are not for sale. In fact, I believe this part of the exhibit is on loan from another museum. But I know of a few galleries in the U.S. that specifically carry African art."

With his hands clasped behind his back, Dane turned slowly until he was now facing her. He was still one hell of a man. Tall —which was actually a relief to Zera considering her own height—broad shoulders, slightly bowed legs, tree bark brown skin and smoldering dark brown eyes. The lightly-trimmed beard was new, but the thick brows and close-cut black hair was the same. The scent of his cologne was different, but still mesmerizing. And his stance was still powerful and domineering. If she were another type of woman, she might be inclined to sigh at the sight of him. Considering she'd never been the type to want and not make every effort to get, she openly admired him without pretense.

He knew she liked what she saw. She could tell by the slight lifting at the corner of his mouth and the way his eyes darkened. Dane appreciated honesty and having a woman ride him until he came. Zera warmed at the memory.

"You would share your connections with me?" he asked, his voice suddenly deeper.

I would have shared my whole world with you.

Those words thankfully remained in her mind.

"Of course," she said. "I actually know a very talented sculptor from Nairobi. He has not been featured at a museum yet. But his work is phenomenal. I will get you his contact information and his website."

"Thanks," Dane replied. "I would appreciate that."

The next moments passed with them staring at each other, wondering which one would act first. This was different, she thought. When they'd met before there was no such contest. Dane acted and she reacted. She acted and he returned in kind. They were combustible from the first moment they met. This time, there'd been a low simmer the moment she'd seen him step away from the ticket booth. Her heart rate had quickened as the decision to stay or leave warred in her mind. Of course she'd stayed.

"We will have to leave," he said. "The museum is closing in fifteen minutes."

Zera lifted an arm and looked at her watch. He was correct. This was not one of the two late nights the museum offered, so they would have to leave. No matter how much she wanted to stay with him. That lack of control was familiar and irritating.

Her response was to begin walking toward the exit. Dane fell into step beside her.

"How long are you staying in Paris?" she asked because she would kick herself the rest of the night if she did not get at least some answers to the questions gnawing at her.

"I booked the hotel for two weeks," he said.

"Business?"

"Vacation," he replied.

She turned to him, unable to mask her surprise. "Dane Donovan is taking a vacation. I do not believe it."

She chuckled and was rewarded by the appearance of a

slow, half smile. They were rare and breath-snatching and Zera was pleased that she'd managed to get one from him before they parted ways.

"It's been a very busy year for me. I thought a break would be good to prepare for the new work on the horizon."

"Oh, new work. What business are you planning to buy this time? Or do you already own the world?" she asked with only a slight bit of humor.

Dane was an ambitious man. He worked hard and tirelessly, to the point she'd once thought he was trying to prove himself to someone. Or possibly to himself.

"I will be sitting on the Board of Directors for Donovan Oilwell International," he said as they passed into the Grande Galerie once more.

"Really?" she asked.

He looked as if he wanted to say something, but a couple brushed past them in their hurry to exit the museum, and he shrugged in response.

"New business ventures are always my goal," he said.

Zera nodded. "I recall."

She was startled momentarily by his next move. His fingers snaked around her wrist as he pulled her to the side, turning her so that her back was to the wall. When their gazes met, he immediately released his hold on her, but did not step back. He was in her personal space and she did not mind that at all. In fact, she lifted a hand, flattening her palm on his chest as if she meant to hold him back, but without applying any pressure.

"What else do you recall, Zera?" he asked, lowering his voice until she almost couldn't hear him.

"Dane," was all she could manage at the moment.

He was staring at her so intently. There was so much she

wanted to say, and more that she knew she could not divulge. She felt trapped. Not by him or his imposing physique. Not by the desire to kiss him, or to wrap her legs around his waist and beg him to take her. But by their world. By everything and everyone around them. By circumstances that she could neither share nor change.

"Do you recall each of those nights we spent together?" His questions continued. "Do you recall how good it felt when we were connected? When I was deep inside you and you were so tight and warm around me?"

Zera licked her lips because that memory had been what got her through on so many of the nights since he'd been gone.

"I remember," she admitted.

A muscle twitched in his jaw.

"Do you remember telling me that you had never felt that way before? That there had never been another to bring you to climax the way I did?"

Why was he doing this? Why here? Why now?

She nodded, unable and unwilling to lie about such a simple and yet soul-searing truth.

"I remember it all, Dane. Every night. Every dinner. Every breakfast you burned and every bath you drew for me," she said, her voice a breathless whisper. "I remember your touch. Your kiss. The way you filled me so completely. I remember it all."

And the memory had nearly killed her.

"Then tell me why," he said solemnly. "Tell me why you chose him over me."

The request caught Zera off guard. She'd expected him to say this four years ago. Not now.

A guard cleared his throat loudly and Zera let her hand fall from Dane's chest.

Dane waited another few seconds before stepping back and away from her. He turned and was walking before she'd completely gathered herself. In moments, she fell into step behind him, not wanting to get closer. Not wanting him to make that request again.

She didn't have to worry. Dane did not say another word to her while they were in the museum. And when they were outside, he asked curtly, "Do you need a ride?"

"I have my own," she replied without thinking.

"Then goodnight," he said before walking away swiftly.

Zera did not curse. She did not cry. And just like four years ago, she did not go after him. Instead, she watched for a few minutes more, until he disappeared in the crowd of people, before turning in the opposite direction and leaving.

Her steps were heavy as she walked, her heart doing a wild dance that crossed between the happiness of seeing him again, the arousal of him being so close and talking about their time together, and the utter disappointment of being unable to stop the inevitable from happening all over again.

CHAPTER 2

The second Dane entered his hotel room his cell phone rang. He quickly pulled the phone from his pant pocket, only to sigh with disappointment as he looked at the screen to see who was calling.

It wasn't Zera.

She did not have his new number, nor did he have hers. They were just two people in this big city who had run into each other at the museum. That somehow did not ring true, but Dane answered his phone rather than continue to think about it.

"Hi, Son. Just checking to make sure you're settling in alright."

"Hey," Dane replied, hesitating at saying the word "dad." "Just came in from an outing. But other than that, all is well."

He closed the door behind him and entered the room, taking a seat in the chair closest to the window. Dane enjoyed looking out at Paris lit up at night. Actually, he had a thing for cityscapes. Paris was one of his favorites. New York City's was another, even though he lived in Upstate New York.

"That's good. Do you have any plans for your time away?"

Bernard Donovan's deep gruff voice sounded over the phone. It was a voice Dane had become accustomed to hearing over the past nine months. The voice of his biological father.

"Nothing in particular," Dane replied. "I have a few business calls to make and the meeting with Roark in a few days."

"That's right," Bernard said. "He's my cousin Gabe's oldest son. Roark's a good one. His father trained him well, so when Gabe passed after the heart attack, Roark was able to step right in and take care of his mother, Maxine. And he made sure Ridge and Suri went to college before joining the company."

Gabriel Donovan was the son of Aaron Donovan. Aaron was the brother of Isaiah Donovan, Dane's grandfather. The Donovans had an intricate family tree that started with a patch of land Dane's great-great grandfather inherited in Gillespie County, Texas in 1908. From there Dane's grandfather Rowan Donovan, along with his brother Charleston struck oil at the Beaumont Ranch and Donovan Oilwell, Inc. was born. Years later, as the Donovan offspring each went their own way across the world, starting families, some continued to work at Donovan Oilwell while others started their own successful businesses.

Dane knew the Donovan family history well. Now, it was time he got to know the family members too.

"I believe Ridge will also be at the meeting," Dane said to Bernard.

"That's good that you're joining forces with the family. This new business venture should work to solidify your rightful place in the family business."

His rightful place. Dane's mother, Roslyn Ausby, used to say that to him in those years that she'd been blackmailing Albert, Henry and Bernard Donovan, over which one of them was Dane's biological father. Roslyn had insisted that Dane was a Donovan and that part of the family's massive fortune belonged to him. Dane had made his own fortune, so finding out who his father was had nothing to do with money as far as he was concerned. The reluctantly taken DNA test had revealed Bernard Donovan as Dane's father. And now they were here, having one of many conversations they'd had in the last nine months. Conversations which were meant to bring father and son closer. Dane was all for making the effort.

"Your brothers have done an exceptional job bringing Donovan Oilwell into the 21st century. And Roark and Ridge have worked tirelessly to achieve the same results for Donovan Oilwell UK. Expanding into the clean air market with a focus on fostering sustainable cities, is a logical next step for the overall Donovan Oilwell brand," Dane said.

It was the same pitch Dane delivered to Roark and the same presentation, Dane and his cousin would make to the executives they'd selected to work at the new Donovan International headquarters in London.

"They're your uncles, Dane," Bernard stated evenly. I'm your father and the Donovans are *your* family."

But only for the last nine months. Before then, Dane's only family had been Roslyn and Jaydon, his younger sister.

"I know," he said, because he did know the truth now. It was still hard digesting all of it—the blackmail, his mother's mental illness which drove her to kill and kidnap in her outrage, his sister's duplicity, and both of their eventual deaths. Not to mention the three men who had slept with his mother and then cohesively denied the child she'd carried. It was a lot to take in. And another reason for the semi-vacation.

"How's Keysa and Madison?" Dane asked in an effort to shift the topic.

Keysa was Bernard's daughter with his first wife Mary Lee Donovan and Madison was Keysa's one year-old daughter.

"They're doing really well. I was in Detroit just last weekend visiting with them. Keysa and Ian are planning a huge Labor Day cookout to make up for everyone who missed Madison's first birthday party. So be sure to keep some time free on your calendar so you won't miss it. I know she'll want you to be there."

"I wouldn't miss it for the world," Dane said. While he was still adjusting to being part of such a large family, the thought of seeing his niece again made Dane smile.

She was a precious little girl who knew nothing about his past or the wrongs his mother or the Senior Donovan men had done. She was innocent and pure and each time she looked up at Dane it was with unconditional love. Something he'd never known in his life.

"Brynne and Wade will travel for the party as well, I presume," Dane said. One thing he'd learned about the Donovan family, even before he'd been accepted into the fold, was that they were a loyal bunch. They supported each other in everything from business ventures outside of the family oilwell, to weddings, baby showers, and now with the 4th generation marrying and having children, birthday parties.

"Yeah, they'll be out. Your youngest sister is doing really well with her new job running the San Francisco branch of the Lakefield Galleries," Bernard said proudly.

Brynne was Bernard's daughter from his second, and now ex-wife, Jocelyn.

"I talked to her just before I left the States," Dane said. "She's looking into a few paintings I was interested in."

"Good. Good," Bernard said. "I'm so glad my children are all coming together."

Dane did not respond.

"You know I've been thinking a lot in these past months," Bernard continued. "Not about the mistakes I've made, because I've apologized for them and I'm dedicated to doing whatever I need to do to make things right in the present. But instead I've been thinking about the future."

Dane held the phone to his ear as he looked out to the evening sky. He slipped a hand into his front pant pocket while he waited for whatever else his father wanted to say.

"I'm thinking about asking Mary Lee out on a date," Bernard said. "I know it's been more than twenty years since we were married. But to be honest, I was always confused by why she left me in the first place. And since Keysa had the baby, I've been going to Detroit more frequently and you know Mary Lee lives there. So I've been seeing her more frequently. Of course, you know, we're connected by our daughter and our grandbaby. But I don't know, the last few times I've been feeling like there may be something more to it."

Was his father asking for his advice? Dane never had any close guy friends to exchange advice on dating or women in general before. He wasn't sure what to say.

"It's silly, huh? Thinking about asking out a woman you were once married to." Bernard chuckled. "I don't know what I was thinking."

"Ask her," Dane said.

"Yeah?"

"Yeah," he continued with a slight grin. "You like her. You

want to take her out on a date. Ask her. What's the worst that can happen?

Bernard chuckled. "She can say no."

Dane shrugged. "Well, she married you once. She had your daughter. Then she left you. Now, you're sharing an adorable granddaughter. Even if she turns down your offer of a date, you still have all that history together."

"Yeah, I guess you've got a point there, Son. "

As he listened to his advice to Bernard, Dane thought of a particular woman that he had history with.

The phone call ended a few minutes later with Dane promising to touch base with Bernard again next week. It was weird to type a date and time to call his father into the calendar on his phone. He'd never had a father to call before. Now, he could admit it felt kind of good.

What didn't feel good was showering and sitting down heavily on the bed with thoughts of Zera Kennedy plaguing him. He'd been successful in keeping her out of his mind—for the most part—over the past years. He'd decided when he boarded that plane and left Paris four years ago that there was no going back. Dane never liked to look back. The future was forward. Always. So he'd tried to forget the betrayal that had cut through his chest like a hot blade. He tried to tamp down the hurt that threatened to take over his every action in those days following her decision to stay with Emmet. And he'd told himself that he would get over it, that it was no big deal.

Seeing her today, Dane had proven himself wrong.

Finding out that Zera was involved with Emmet Parks had been a huge deal. It had crushed any ideas that Dane had about being in a personal relationship with a woman. But today he'd touched her. He'd been so close to her that he could smell the sweet scent of her perfume. He'd listened to her speak, her tone heavy with the African accent that was her heritage. He'd looked at her and remembered every time he'd touched or tasted her.

And now he was damned. Again.

Switching off the lights he lay back against the pillows and closed his eyes. But even that didn't work. He still saw her, still heard her voice. And when he inhaled deeply, he could smell her once again. His body hardened, his mind blocking out everything but her and the glorious two months they'd spent together.

He wanted Zera Kennedy. Again.

He still wasn't sure if she wanted him.

Zera drove through the wet streets of the city, turning and detouring, making her ride home last much longer than it needed to. Rain splashed against the windshield and rolled down the side windows. It was a torrential drenching, one which seemed to fit well with the stormy mood brewing inside of her.

She still couldn't believe she'd run into Dane, after all this time. The decision to visit The Louvre this evening had been an impulsive one. She'd spent the day inside her apartment as she had so many days before. But as the afternoon dragged on and the pity party she'd been deeply ensconced in since January became repugnant, she'd decided that some fresh air was a good idea. Did she somehow know that he was going to be there? Of course that was ridiculous. She could not have known. She hadn't spoken to Dane since the day he'd left her standing beside Emmet at Emmet's New Year's Eve party.

Emmet had reserved the entire Four Seasons George V

resort—meaning he was able to transform every event space in the resort into a private celebratory oasis for New Year's Eve and New Year's Day. Zera recalled the amount of money it had taken to secure the venue, catering and transportation for most of Emmet's more important associates. It had been exorbitant, but then she'd expected nothing less of him.

She wore the off-the-shoulder form-fitting red dress, with its sheer train hanging down to the floor that Emmet had delivered to her the night before. The dress barely skimmed her upper thighs and made her feel way more exposed than if everyone in the room had known where she'd come from and why she was truly there. Revealing dresses weren't her favorite, but she'd known Emmet for almost three months at that time, and already she'd surmised that he did not like being disappointed. And the people who were foolish enough to disappoint him didn't care for Emmet's reaction to whatever they'd done to displease them. Probably because they ended up injured, maimed, or dead.

The ballroom she was in had been decorated in gold, silver and black. Lavish centerpieces of gold candles dangling off the ends of black branches that had been stuffed into tall crystal vases on each table. On black linen covered tables, paper top hats were stacked in pyramids and ropes of beads lay haphazardly. Flutes full of champagne filled silver trays that were carried by servers who walked around the room for easy access. A DJ played everything from Hip Hop to Pop, and during dinner, Jazz. Zera stood near the doors leading to the patio, one arm crossing her waist as she held her nearly empty glass of champagne in the other hand.

"I've been looking for you," Emmet had said from behind her.

She hadn't heard him approach and wouldn't berate herself

for the lapse in attention either. There were at least three hundred people in this ballroom and the music was blasting. That was a justifiable excuse, but the real reason she hadn't heard Emmet was because she'd been too busy thinking of another man.

"I'm right here," she'd replied in a voice void of her African accent. "I figured you would be making your rounds and I didn't want to disturb you."

That had been partially true.

"You could never be a disturbance," Emmet had continued as he trailed the tips of his fingers along the bare skin of her shoulder.

His touch made her feel weird. It hadn't when she'd first met him, but in the past two months another man's touch had brought new life to Zera's body. There was no comparison, so enduring Emmet's touch was a little harder to stand. But she did. There was no other choice.

"And I'd actually like you to meet someone," Emmet had continued.

Zera relaxed enough to smile as she finally turned completely toward where Emmet stood. The action caused his hand to fall from her shoulder, but Emmet immediately turned so that he was now standing beside her. His arm went around her waist as he pulled her close to his side. Then she saw the man Emmet wanted her to meet and her smile faltered.

Her body tensed and dread instantly filled her stomach.

"Here she is, Dane. The woman who has me caught under her seductive spell," Emmet said, his hand moving lower so that his fingers were now splayed over her hip. "Zera, my sweet, this is Dane Donovan. He's an old college friend from America, spending the holidays in our beautiful city."

She'd swallowed and then cleared her throat, stalling for time to figure out what she was going to say. What could she say?

The night before she'd been naked and in bed with Dane. Tonight she was wearing a barely-there dress and standing next to Emmet. She knew how bad it looked, and if she wasn't smart enough to figure that out, the look of disappointment followed by disgust on Dane's face confirmed it.

Dane had spoken first.

"Hello, Zera. It's a pleasure to meet you," he'd said. "Emmet hasn't been able to stop talking about you."

Her heart thumped wildly against her chest as her fingers clenched the stem of the glass she held. *Say something!* Her mind screamed those two words over and over again, until she felt like an idiot for remaining silent.

"It's very nice to meet a longtime friend of Emmet's," she finally managed. "How long will you be staying in Paris, Dane?"

What she really wanted to know was if she'd be able to meet up with him later to explain what was happening. She desperately needed to talk to Dane alone, to tell him…what? How was she going to explain this to him without jeopardizing her and Hiari's life?

"I'm actually flying out first thing tomorrow morning," Dane had replied smoothly. "And if you two will excuse me, there's a phone call I need to make before the new year rings in."

Emmet had chuckled. "Gotta call your lady, huh? I told you it wasn't normal for her not to be on your arm. No matter how new the relationship is, if the woman is special to you, she should be with you at all times. That's why I keep my lovely Zera, close."

As if to punctuate his words, Emmet pulled her closer to him

—if that were even possible. The scent of his cologne almost choked her and she could feel the gun holster he wore beneath his tuxedo jacket.

"You are absolutely right," Dane stated, his gaze locked on hers. "Perhaps my lady friend is not as special as I thought she was."

Zera wanted to cry. Well, not really. Tears were not something she allowed often. It showed a vulnerability she couldn't afford to share with anyone. Still, a part of her felt as if it were crumbling at Dane's words. She began to pant as it became harder to breathe.

With one final look of disdain, Dane turned his attention to Emmet and extended his hand forward.

"Great party, my friend," Dane said to Emmet. "Next time I'm on this side of the pond, I'll be sure to get in touch with you sooner."

"You do that," Emmet replied as he accepted Dane's hand for a shake.

Emmet released his hold on Zera to lean in and embrace Dane before saying, "Safe travels, bro."

"Thanks, man. You be good over here," Dane replied as he pulled back.

"Zera," Dane said tightly. "It was a pleasure."

"Yes," she replied in a breathy whisper. "A pleasure."

Because it had been. Every second of the last sixty days that she'd spent with him had been new and refreshing, passionate and rewarding, and something Zera hadn't wanted to lose. But she had, she'd thought as she watched Dane walk away. She knew that she'd lost him and there hadn't been anything she could do to prevent that from happening.

Even now, four years later, her heart still hurt with that

thought. She slammed her palm on the steering wheel cursing the tears that threatened to spill. There had been no point in crying over Dane Donovan back then and there certainly wasn't one now. Nothing had changed. Her reasons for not telling him the truth back then were only exemplified now. Emmet may be dead, but Hiari was still missing. And as long as that was the case, Zera wasn't free to pursue any type of relationships. Even the delectably physical one she'd once shared with Dane.

It was almost eleven by the time Zera finally pulled into the car park where she routinely parked her car. Two days after Emmet's death, she'd moved out of his luxury apartment in le Figaro with the bag of cash she knew he kept in a locked trunk at the back of his closet. There was a mixture of U.S. Dollars and Euros and after she'd booked herself a hotel room, Zera had taken the time to count it all. The total was 1.5 million. One month later, Zera checked out of the hotel and signed a lease for a studio apartment in the Heart of St. Germain, in Paris's 6th Arrondissement located on the River Seine. Zera loved this area which had a reputation for being the home to famous artists and writers. For her, it was the charming streets, historic architecture, and antique shops that held her attention. It was the calm to the never-ending storm of her reality.

The rain had slowed to a quiet drizzle and she huddled beneath her small umbrella as she speed-walked down the block to her building. It dawned on her at that moment that she actually looked a mess and had looked this way when she'd seen the one man that actually made her give a damn about her looks. Dane was the absolute last person she'd expected to see when she'd decided to step outside earlier this evening. So the black polka dot tennis shoes, black yoga pants and gray half zip shirt from her college alma mater—Tuskegee University—she wore would now be the last thing he remembered seeing her in. She'd left her hair loose because she'd felt like styling it and she wore no make-up or accessories. Still, Dane had come close enough to almost kiss her.

The memory of how close they'd been inside the museum warmed her even as the chilly rain continued to fall. Snapping the umbrella closed and ducking into the small lobby area of the building, Zera shivered. She raced up the single flight of stairs and down a short hallway to the door of her apartment. Pulling her key from the chain she wore around her neck and had tucked into her shirt, she unlocked the door, stepped inside and froze.

Something wasn't right.

Zera was certain she had switched off all the lights when she'd left the apartment earlier, but now, the overhead hanging lamp near her desk was on. She moved very slowly, bending her knees until she was in a squatting position. Her eyes continued to scan the room as her hand moved to lift her right pant leg. The bed was about six feet across from the desk. The traditional handmade Maasai quilt her grandmother had given her when she'd moved away to college was still neatly smoothed over the queen-size mattress. A short distance to the left was her kitchen. The tea kettle and mug she'd used before leaving were still on the counter. But next to it now lay a long-stemmed white rose.

Zera unsnapped the sheath just above her ankle and slowly slid the knife out of its holder. She gripped the handle in the palm of her hand and came to a stand. On the other side of her bed, a dresser and two barrel chairs were against the orange painted wall with two windows. Both windows were still closed, raindrops peppering the glass. She looked up—not that she expected an intruder to be above her clinging to one of the thick dark brown beams that crossed from one side of the room to the next, but just as a precaution. Moving quietly Zera checked the closet and then the bathroom. Returning to the main room of the apartment she looked around again before falling to her knees and pushing the dust ruffle up so she could peek under the bed.

This time when she stood Zera sighed loudly before sitting on the side of the bed. She still held the knife and finally lowered the hand it was in to rest on her thigh.

It was starting.

Again.

CHAPTER 3

*D*ebare Adebayo dropped to his knees and pulled the black lockbox he traveled with from beneath the bed in his hotel room. With a key he kept on a rope tied around his ankle, he opened the box and retrieved his gun and $7500 in cash. Closing the box and pushing it under the bed, he lifted the sweatshirt he wore and tucked the wads of cash into the waistband of his jeans. He stood and checked the gun for bullets, before slipping that into the back of his pants and pulling his sweatshirt down.

He grabbed his cell phone off the bed where he'd dropped it when he came in a few minutes ago, and checked for messages. None.

Debare shook his head. He had no doubt that sonofabitch would make contact tonight. He could feel it in his bones. Cursing, Debare went to the windows and yanked the string that would close the blinds. It didn't seem to completely work as a gap in the center remained open for anyone to see through.

Anyone meaning, the person that he was certain had been hired to kill him.

That's how they worked. You either did what they said, gave them everything they wanted, or died. There were no other options. And Debare had failed. Sort of.

Moving into the bathroom, Debare retrieved the backpack he'd hung on the hook behind the door. It fell from his hand and he swore while bending down to pick it up. This wasn't how this was supposed to go.

He'd done everything that was asked of him, including some things that were repercussions of the decision he'd made.

Debare was born to be a king. His father had told him that from the time he could walk. He was meant to rule, to own land and to live prosperously in Ongata Rongai, the area in Nairobi where his family was from. But after his father became sick and suddenly died from an incurable disease, Debare's world took a dramatic turn. He was no longer the next in line to inherit his father's land, as that land was taken from them by the financial institutions that assisted in keeping their people in a state of suffrage. Months later his mother had worked herself to the point of sickness and combined with the grief of losing his father, succumbed as well, leaving sixteen year-old Debare on his own.

Believing there was nothing for him in the region, Debare left Nairobi and ended up in Nigeria, where he met a man named Abu. That meeting changed Debare's life and for a while, Debare thought it had been changed for the better.

Tightening his grip on the bag, Debare pushed the bathroom door open once more and took a step into the room. It was the last step he would ever take.

The hand grabbed his neck quickly, pulling him further into

the room as he sputtered to speak. He was tossed onto the floor, the backpack falling from his fingers. Looking up into the face covered by black cloth wrapped completely around the intruder's head so that only the eyes were revealed, Debare attempted to scoot across the carpeted floor. He pushed a hand behind his back and had just grabbed the handle of his gun when the glint of the machete's blade came down quickly.

What was she doing?

This was foolish and Zera knew it.

Yesterday was a chance meeting. It wasn't anything like fate or some old African proverb her mother and grandmother would recite. The world was a big place, if two people could meet among billions and experience sixty days of unimaginable pleasure, then it was just as likely that those same two people could meet again four years later. Right? There was nothing strange going on here—at least nothing that had to do with Dane.

The fact that she'd awakened earlier than usual this morning and immediately resumed her search for what Dane had been doing this past year, why he might be back in Paris and—most importantly—where he was staying, was not a result of her still pining for this man. She'd had him, so there was no curiosity to appease. He had been the one to leave so there should have been no guilt to carry. Now, he was back and they'd managed to be very civil to one another. All was well.

And still, hours after she'd first logged onto her computer, Zera continued to search.

There had been some trauma in Dane's life since she'd last

seen him. His mother had died. Stock in Imagine Energy Corporation maintained stability, even in the U.S.'s present economic state. There were pictures of him at a beautiful double wedding in Napa Valley and then months later at an economic development summit in Washington, D.C. In every picture he looked the same. No, that wasn't true. If it were humanly possible, he actually looked better. Whether he was wearing a tuxedo, designer suit or jeans and a blazer, Dane Donovan was a very attractive man.

It was a wonder that had not been the first thing that pulled Zera to him. When they'd met at The Louvre four years ago, she'd been far more attracted to his keen eye for detail and how he'd been drawn to the same types of art that she'd always admired. His voice, the build of his body, the ease with which he moved into a space and totally dominated it with his presence, was just icing on the cake. And after two dinner dates, when she'd willingly joined him in his hotel room and eagerly lay in that bed beside him, she knew she was hooked. There was nothing she'd wanted more than to wake up next to him every morning and fall asleep beside him every night.

Nothing, except to find Hiari.

Her younger cousin had been kidnapped from school in Samburu, just about five years ago. Zera made a vow to her family that she would find her and that she would not return to Kenya without her. All these years later that declaration still weighed heavily on Zera's heart. She believed that Hiari was still alive. She had to believe it. If not, she would have let her entire family down and that wasn't something Zera thought she could live with.

Dane was staying at the Novotel Paris Centre Tour Eiffel. Zera smiled as the reservation finally popped up on her screen.

One of her well-hidden talents was hacking. It was illegal, no matter which country she was in, which was why she'd never shared with anyone that she was so good at it. Novotel wasn't the most high-end hotel in Paris. Zera had graced the majority of them during her time with Emmet, and she was certain that Dane could have afforded much better. She wondered why he was staying there, just as she still had not found out why he was here.

Well, she decided after shutting down her computer, she was going to get some answers. And she was going to give him an explanation for what happened all those years ago. Of course it wasn't going to be the total truth, it couldn't be, even now. Especially now. But she felt like she had to say something. She did not have the opportunity back then, and she wanted to now. Hopefully, if she could at least get some of this off her chest, she could finally move on from him. Hopefully.

Zera waited in the lobby for two hours. She'd read newspapers, went into the café to grab a cup of coffee and then returned to the lobby to wait a while longer. Slipping 25 euros to a member of the cleaning staff alerted her to the fact that Dane was still in the room. Now, it was just about three in the afternoon, he would have to leave his room at some point.

She rubbed a finger over the rim of the now empty cup and kept her gaze focused on the bank of elevators. Why didn't she just board an elevator and go to his room? Would that make her look desperate or slightly insane? If Dane wanted her to know where he was staying, wouldn't he have told her last night? Wouldn't he have invited her back to his room as he'd done years ago?

Questions rolled through her mind like a busy subway train. Her phone was in her front pocket on vibrate. She resisted the urge to pull it out and check the time again. Maybe she should find another cleaning person and ask them to check Dane's room again. Maybe he'd slipped out while she'd been at the café.

Maybe this was ridiculous and she should just get up and go back to her apartment. She had more than enough to do there. Staking out Dane Donovan just so she could tell him a partial truth as to why she'd let him walk out of her life with no explanation wasn't a priority. Or at least it shouldn't be. Not for her. But for Dane? He'd asked her last night why she'd chosen Emmet over him and the look in his eyes as he'd waited for that answer said he really wanted to know. He deserved to know.

Zera inhaled deeply and stood as she exhaled. She went to a trashcan near the front desk and reached into her pocket for her phone. She would call Dane's room and tell him that she was downstairs waiting to see him. If he still wanted to talk, she was here. If he didn't. She would go. But when she looked up again, it was to see him stepping off the elevator.

He wore black jeans today and a gray shirt that molded against his toned chest. Sunglasses, a silver ring worn on his right hand, and black tie-up leather shoes completed his ensemble. The slow and steady gait was his signature and the sight of him so close and yet still so emotionally far away, had her heart beating faster.

It was now or never, Zera thought as she watched him walking toward the front entrance. She stuffed her phone back into her pocket and moved across the lobby. When he was just a couple steps in front of her, she called his name.

He stopped and turned and her breath caught as she almost stumbled right into his broad chest.

"Hello," she said, taking a step back.

Zera tucked wayward strands of hair behind her ears and smiled tentatively.

"Hello," he replied and reached up to remove his sunglasses from his face. "Are you staying at this hotel too?"

"No," she said with a shake of her head. "I wanted to talk to you. To finish the conversation you started last night."

For what seemed like endless moments, Dane only stared at her. She wanted him to say something and then thought that perhaps she should do all the talking. After all, she was the one with the answers.

"It's over," he said finally. "Four years is a long time and we've both lived a lot of life since then. It was really great seeing you again, but we can both walk away with a clear conscience."

He attempted to turn away as he'd done last night, but this time, Zera grabbed his arm. The touch sent bolts of fire through her fingers and up her arm. The warmth threatened to draw her closer to him, to lean into him the way she had before.

"My conscience isn't clear," Zera said.

Dane might never know how true those four words really were for her. But she continued, "I want to answer your question. To say some things that I did not get a chance to say four years ago."

His brow creased. "It doesn't matter now."

"I think it does," she said. "At least to me. And probably to you, since you didn't hesitate bringing it up last night."

A woman bumped into her, mumbling "excuse me" as she passed by. Dane took her hand from his arm and pulled her alongside him as he walked toward the hotel restaurant. Once at the entrance he spoke perfect French, requesting a table for two near the window. The hostess happily obliged and in seconds they were being led to a table. Dane pulled the chair out for her and Zera took a seat. She waited until he'd done the same across from her before speaking again.

"You wanted to know why I chose Emmet over you," she said when the hostess had left them alone with menus. "I didn't."

Dane had been holding the menu and looking down at it. Now, he stared at her and set the menu on the table.

"I left the party that night and flew home, alone, the next morning. My initial plan that day had been to bring in the new year with you. But you did not answer my calls all day. When I arrived at Emmet's party, I found out why," Dane told her.

"You misunderstood," she said.

"Emmet said you were his woman. He'd been speaking highly of a new woman in his life since earlier in the week. One who was making him rethink everything he'd thought he wanted in life. One who was going to change his world. That woman was you."

He said the last as if the words actually pained him to release. For Zera, they were hard to hear, especially coming from Dane. She'd never wanted to be Emmet's woman. But she'd had no other choice. Would Dane understand that?

"Emmet was a means to an end. An assignment I needed to complete," she said hoping the latter would make up for how the first explanation may have sounded. "I was there at his party that night to do a job."

Dane shook his head. "What type of job has you posing as another man's woman? What type of job puts you in that man's bed at night?"

"I was not in his bed at night," she countered.

"No," Dane said with a slight nod. "You were in mine."

A waitress brought them glasses of water. Zera sat back in her chair and Dane ordered for himself. On a nod from her, he requested the same meal for her.

"This is not how I envisioned this conversation going," she said after a few moments.

"I never envisioned this conversation," he stated evenly.

Zera gritted her teeth. She'd known this wasn't going to be easy. She hadn't guessed that Dane's clipped and accusatory tone would be so painful.

"Emmet is dead," he said before she could think of how she wanted to approach the rest of the conversation. "You said so yourself and last night I tried calling the numbers I'd had for him and even called the company he'd mentioned freelancing for the last time I'd seen him, but he was nowhere to be found. So I guess that's it."

"You didn't believe me?"

He ignored her question.

"We went to college together, but we weren't the best of friends. I don't subscribe to personal relationships of that sort. You did your thing and I did mine. So let's just end it there."

She flattened her hands on the table and stared at him. "But I have more to say."

"If it's on the same subject, save it. You don't owe me any explanations. I shouldn't have asked that question last night. From this moment on I don't give a damn what other man you've been with. Let's just enjoy our late lunch and move on."

It sounded like a command and Zera did not like that. She'd been trained to take orders, and normally, she did so without too much qualm. But this time she felt like she should push back a little more. She should fight to say the words, only what words was she going to say? When she'd decided to come here she'd known that she wouldn't be able to tell Dane the full truth. She'd planned to adjust her story so that it still contained her main theme—that she would never in a million years have voluntarily chosen Emmet over Dane. Now, he was telling her that none of that was necessary. If Zera knew what was best for her, she would take that and run with it.

Zera didn't count herself a fool.

"I could eat a late lunch," she said.

"Fine," Dane replied.

Dane was through with secrets being revealed. He was tired of things from the past coming back to bite a person in the ass. And the very last thing he wanted to hear or think about was Zera being with Emmet, regardless of the reason. He just did not want to know.

They enjoyed the chicken pad thai and the scenery and basically ate in silence. There were things Dane had planned to do today, but this morning's emergency conference call with representatives from his San Francisco office had altered his schedule. The fact that at the time, it was close to midnight in California, Dane had known the call was urgent and so had not argued too much about taking it. Hours later the issue had been settled and he was able to finally shower and get ready for the day. Thoughts of Zera had ceased at that point.

He hadn't dreamed about her, but then, Dane rarely dreamed. He had never been one to dream, or at least he'd never recalled said dreams when he woke in the morning. That could have been considered a good thing since, as it turned out, his life had been pretty eventful so far. But he had sat at that table near the window in his room where he'd stood last night talking to Bernard, and thought about the woman who was now sitting across from him.

Today she looked refreshed and prettier than ever. Her high cheekbones and pert lips just a part of her overall allure. She'd left her hair out again today, but this time had added a little curl to the even-cut strands. Jeans fit her long slender legs perfectly, while the breezy material of her sleeveless lavender blouse crisscrossed over medium-size breasts. She wore no rings on her fingers and only a chocolate-colored leather bracelet on her right wrist.

"Are you here for business or pleasure?"

Her voice snatched Dane from his thoughts and he sipped on the last of the beer he'd ordered before replying.

"A little of both," he told her.

"Tell me about your business," she said.

He frowned. "Why do you want to know?"

"Because I'm tired of sitting at this table in uncomfortable silence," she replied.

When he only stared at her she hunched her shoulders for a look that was both innocent and sexy at the same time. Dane cleared his throat and used a napkin to wipe his mouth one last time.

"I am starting a new business venture. Preliminary meetings have taken place long distance so far and now it is time to put things into motion. For that, I needed to be here," he said.

"Oh, so you'll now have a division of your company here in Paris?"

What did she know about his company, Dane wondered.

When he had been here before, that was not something they talked about. In fact, they hadn't talked much about anything the other was involved in—whether business or pleasure—when they'd been together before. They'd only talked about the moment, the surprise, and delight of it all.

"In a way. It's more like a new partnership with...my cousins," he said after a slight hesitation. Dane still wasn't used to claiming all this family he now had.

Zera folded her arms and rested them on the table in front of her. She leaned in a little close as she nodded. "In what area of business?"

"Energy conservation," he said and smiled up at the waitress who set the black folder with their check on the edge of the table beside him.

Zera reached into her pocket. "Let me get my wallet," she was saying.

Dane had already pulled his from his back pant pocket and was tucking his credit card into the folder.

"Put your money away," he said with slight irritation.

Did she really think he would make her pay for her food?

"This is not a date," she quickly countered.

"It is not," he agreed. "But I think I can pay a lunch tab after you went to all the trouble to find me."

She slipped her small wallet back into her pocket and tilted her head as she stared at him. "It was no trouble."

He raised a brow. "I didn't tell you which hotel I was staying in, so you had to figure that out somehow."

"I have friends in the hospitality industry here in the city. It was just a matter of making a few phone calls," she replied.

Dane wasn't so sure he liked knowing he could be found in just a few phone calls. Then again, it wasn't as if he was on some secret mission. Nor was he hiding from anyone, so he dismissed the issue.

"Nevertheless, I can pay for your meal. Next time, however, it'll be your treat."

He had no idea why he'd said that last part. Was there even going to be a next time? Seeing Zera last night was a surprise, hearing her call his name a little while ago, another shock. But would they see each other again? No.

"Sure," she replied quickly. "How about breakfast tomorrow? I recall you have a fondness for French pastries."

She recalled? Dane did not want to think of the things she recalled about their time together. He didn't want to admit that his memory of those days and nights were also crystal clear in his mind.

"I have meetings all morning and into the afternoon tomorrow."

Was that disappointment he saw quickly flash over her face?

"That's fine. If you have a moment to do some sightseeing before you leave, let me know. I mean, since we have cleared the air between us, there is no reason why I cannot play tour guide for you."

None except every second that he was near her was like a sweet type of torture. The kind that a man could be truly enticed by because he knew the end game would be worth it. Dane did not have time for torture of any kind. Especially not by way of a female relationship.

"How about dinner? I can pick you up at seven," he said, again shocking himself.

She smiled and Dane's shock withered away, to be replaced by warmth that spread quickly throughout his body. She had a brilliant smile that showcased straight white teeth and touched her eyes with just a hint of light.

"That sounds fantastic," she replied. "Dinner tomorrow at seven."

Yes, Dane thought. He was going to have dinner with Zera and then that would be it. He would continue his trip, handle his business and return to the States inside the two-week window which he'd allotted. That would be all.

But as they stood and walked out of the restaurant together, Dane thought differently. His gaze shifted to the sway of her hips as she walked in front of him. When they stepped outside of the hotel, a warm breeze had the scent of her perfume wafting up to his nose and filtering through his body. She extended her hand for him to shake and he thought it was the silliest thing considering all they'd been through. But it was smart, and still, the supposed casual contact only added to the brewing arousal he'd been trying valiantly to deny.

"Tomorrow at seven, I will pick you up," he told her and reached into his pocket to retrieve his cell phone. "Give me your number and address."

Zera pulled out her phone as well. She rattled off her number and then paused.

"I will meet you," she said. "I have business to tend to tomorrow as well so it may be easier to just meet at a restaurant."

Dane raised a brow as the thought of her not wanting him to know where she lived entered his mind. It was quickly dismissed as inconsequential. There was no need for him to know. None at all.

"I will text you once I make the reservations," he said and then gave her his number.

"Great," she replied.

"Yeah, great," he said, and because Dane considered himself a man of action, he ignored all the bullshit he'd fed himself during their meal together.

He stepped closer to Zera, wrapping his arm around her slim waist and pulled her hard against him. The kiss was also hard and urgent, a quick punch of need that he had to get out of his system. His lips pressed against hers, his tongue not waiting for an invite, but pushing through to tangle quickly and hotly with hers.

It was enough, Dane told himself as he let her go and broke the kiss with no more warning than he'd given her about it in the first place. He stepped back, enjoying the look of aroused confusion on her face for only a moment, before he turned to walk away.

He could still do that, Dane thought as he continued down the street without looking back. He could walk away from Zera Kennedy with his world intact. He'd done it before and he was glad to know he could do so again.

CHAPTER 4

*D*ane Donovan's net worth was $300 million. This included $42 million in Donovan Oilwell stock he'd acquired in the last three years. So it should have been no surprise to Zera when he met her at the lot where she'd parked her car and escorted her to the dock on the Ile de la Cité. She tamped down on awe and giddiness as he stepped on board the shiny yacht and held out his hand to help her onto the deck as well. Once aboard, Dane nodded to the driver and walked them down to the lower deck.

"Have a seat," he said in a deep gruff voice and motioned to the white leather bench seats that stretched along one side of the vessel.

She did and, regardless of the top-of-the-line elegant décor, kept her gaze focused on Dane. This evening he wore charcoal gray slacks, leather loafers, and a lighter gray chambray shirt. His short beard was freshly trimmed, chest broad and defined even through the material of his shirt.

"When you asked me to dinner tonight, I didn't think you

would go to this much trouble," she remarked as he was fixing them both a drink.

Zera hadn't considered they would be sharing a meal on a yacht, but she had enough experience with this particular man to know that wearing the long flowing red skirt, short-sleeved white bodysuit and red striped sandals was a good idea. Dane didn't do anything half-assed. He dressed impeccably, whether it was a designer tuxedo or jeans and four thousand dollar tie-up shoes. And he looked great in everything. Zera especially recalled how the boxer briefs he used to wear molded over the thick cheeks of his tight ass. She'd been thinking about those boxer briefs a lot in the past three days.

"Well, since I had to call you the other day to cancel our first dinner. Then could only manage two quick lunches with you in the last couple of days, I figured I owed you," he said and then handed her a glass.

Zera sipped the red wine and smiled. She'd told him that she preferred red yesterday when they'd debated what the appropriate time of day to have wine was. To her way of thinking the answer was all day, every day. Dane preferred after five. It was almost eight now and she noticed he'd fixed himself a glass of whiskey.

"You don't owe me anything," she said and then took another sip from her glass. "I mean, we both have lives we're living."

"True," Dane replied and took a seat on the opposite side of the bench.

If they weren't alone, at least four people could fit into the space he'd left between them. Zera tried not to think too much into that. She shouldn't be thinking too much into any of this, but that was much easier said than done.

She finished her wine and he finished his drink.

"Dinner will be served in twenty minutes," he told her. "You'll like it. I selected a few things that I recalled you enjoyed."

"You remembered what I liked to eat," she said. Sometimes Zera's candor was problematic. But it had been said, so she looked at him expecting a response.

He stared down at his empty glass for a few moments, before standing and setting it on the bar across from them. When he turned around again, he looked at her and gave that small smile that was way too charismatic for any one man to possess.

"While I remember our past, I'd rather stay focused on the present," he replied.

She nodded. "Okay. I can work with that."

"Can you?" he asked and then stepped closer to her.

He knelt down in front of her and Zera's fingers tightened on the stem of her glass.

"I can…do anything," she said. The flash of a scene from her childhood when her grandmother had made her recite those very words came with such potency that the glass wobbled in her hand.

"Then you need to decide if we're doing this," he continued.

Zera wished she hadn't finished her drink. Her fingers moved over the glass. She wanted to shake, but fear was not an option. Besides, there was nothing to fear. Dane would never hurt her and whatever he was proposing obviously required a yes or no answer.

"Are we doing what, Dane?" she asked before standing. For a second he was still on his knee in front of her, his face perfectly aligned with her center. It throbbed in response and she pressed her thighs as tightly together as she could manage without being obvious. Seconds later, Zera was moving around him. She went to the bar and refilled her glass, taking a sip before turning back to face him.

He had moved so that he was now sitting on the bench again, his legs spread apart, hands resting on his muscled thighs.

"Starting another affair," he said as simply as if he'd just given her a weather report.

Zera took another sip because the sight of him sitting there in a position that was clearly inviting her to straddle him, take him, take them both to the pleasure she'd so desperately missed, was making her throat dry.

"I don't do affairs anymore," she replied finally because it was the right answer.

In the past few days since Dane had been in Paris, Zera had thought about almost nothing but him and what they'd had four years ago. She recalled every second of those days and nights and experienced that same ache in her chest that she'd had on New Year's Eve when she watched him walk away. It had felt so fresh and so intense that she'd vowed never to put herself in that position again. It was too much. Combined with everything else going on in her life, it was enough to push her over the brink. Zera wasn't about to let that happen.

"What else have you got to offer?" she asked Dane, already knowing his answer.

Dane didn't do forever either. He'd said as much when they were together before. Zera was banking on that position to have remained the same.

"Just this," he said and lifted his arms so that it appeared he was offering himself.

Oh, that was so tempting. Having Dane Donovan again was more tempting than the thought of giving her mother her greatest wish and returning to Nairobi. Zera knew instinctively that she couldn't afford to do either one.

"That's good," she said, purposely making her voice lighter to take the sexual tension now filling the air away. "But I'll pass."

She was finishing off her second glass of wine when he chuckled.

"Okay," he said and then shrugged. "That's cool. I'll be here another week and a half. Let me know if you change your mind. In the meantime, let's have dinner."

"Great idea. I'm starving," she said as she watched him stand and head back up the steps that would take them to the deck.

She was tempted to fix herself another glass of wine. This time she would fill it to the rim and down it in one continuous gulp so that it could hit her fast and hard. Perhaps she needed to fill her glass with whiskey instead. Anything to convince herself that she was doing the right thing and that she could actually resist falling into bed with Dane again.

Zera knew she had to resist.

So many lives depended on her staying focused this time. And once she let Dane back into her heart, Zera knew just how vulnerable she would be. Not only was another affair with Dane Donovan not smart, this time it could prove deadly.

Sailing the Seine at night was almost as beautiful as watching Zera sit on the bench on deck, her arms wrapped around legs pulled up to her chest, the yellow polish on her toenails twinkling in the dark. It was a breezy evening and her hair wafted up from her neck to blow in the wind. She looked both angelic and sexy simultaneously and in that moment, Dane knew that he wanted her. It was that simple and that complex. He wanted this woman in a way he'd never wanted before.

That was strange because he'd actually already had her, more than once. As angry as Dane had been with her when he'd left Paris four years ago, he'd always cherished the memories they'd made together. Probably because he'd never shared peanut butter and jelly on croissants or nights listening to the bluesy tones of Miles Davis with any other woman. Or perhaps it was because finding his release while buried deep inside Zera had been better than being with all the women he'd had prior, and after, those two months he'd spent in Paris.

What was even more perplexing was the fact that she'd not only told him no, but that he was still feeling a bit annoyed by it.

"I love sailing," she said. "The air is different on the water. Fresher and cleaner. And I love the sound of the waves. I mean, of course we're not hearing any crashing waves on the Seine, but out on the ocean, it's such a soothing sound."

"I'd rather fly, or drive a really fast car," Dane admitted.

"Really? What type of car do you drive when you are at home?"

She tilted her head so that she was looking over to where he stood at the railing. He'd been leaning against it, hands stuffed in his front pockets as he'd stared at her.

"I have a few vehicles in New York," he told her. "A Jaguar X Type, BMW Alpina, a Cadillac XTS sedan and an Escalade. The Jaguar is, of course, the fastest. But I don't get to drive it much."

"Right, because you're probably being picked up in a limo and chauffeured around all the time," she said.

Dane paused before replying, wondering if that was

bitterness or sarcasm he heard in that statement. "I do have a driver who uses the sedan to drive me to work, but only because driving in the city isn't my favorite pastime. Other than that, I drive myself. Especially when I'm in San Francisco. I enjoy the scenery there."

She nodded. "That's right, you have more than one house."

"You've done your research on me," he said. "I know because you figured out where I was staying. Tell me what else you know."

She leaned in closer, resting her chin on her knees and Dane wanted to walk over and touch the skin of her cheek.

"You're forty-one years old, and will celebrate your forty-second birthday in November. You graduated from Harvard with honors before returning to Harvard Business School and obtaining a masters. You also own a private jet—a Gulfstream G650, three houses and one beach house in Bali. But no pets." She narrowed her eyes at him and shook her head. "What's the matter, you don't like pets, Dane?"

"It's a commitment," he replied instantly. "You've retained all that information as if you were preparing some type of report. You have a great memory."

She shrugged and said, "Sometimes."

Dane continued watching her as she unwrapped her arms from around her knees and turned on the bench. Her legs straightened and her bare feet touched the glossed wood floor of the deck. She stood up and stretched her arms above her head. Her breasts pressed into the thin white material of her top and his fingers itched to touch them.

"What time is it? It feels like it's pretty late," she said, when her stretch was over and her arms fell to her side.

He pulled his hands from his pockets and looked at the watch on his wrist. "Just a little after eleven."

"Wow. We've been out here a while," she said and took a step toward where she'd left her shoes.

"Time flies," Dane said before quickly closing the space between them.

He had his hands on her waist in seconds, holding her still in front of him. Her hands gripped his biceps, probably more out of instinct than desire. But when she looked up at him Dane wasn't so sure. Her gaze was dark, her lips slightly parted.

"I want to kiss you," Dane said by way of asking permission.

He waited a beat for her response and when none came, he lowered his head until his lips brushed lightly over hers. Zera's fingers tightened on his biceps and Dane groaned because that was, no doubt, an act of desire. He touched her lips once more, just a whisper of his over hers. She didn't pull away. She didn't whisper a no or curse him for taking liberties. So he touched his tongue to her bottom lip and felt her lean closer into him. He licked the seam of her lips, the corners and then over the plump bottom lip again. She held on to him tightly. He slipped his arms around her waist, cradling her body against his as he tilted his head and touch his tongue to her lips again.

"Let me in," he whispered over her mouth.

She was staring at him, her long lashes fluttering as she tried to keep from closing her eyes.

"Again," she sighed as she opened her mouth to him.

His tongue was on hers instantly, a soft, warm touch before the long slow swipe that re-ignited the heat that had never died between them. Her arms moved quickly, up and around his neck, her palms flattening on the back of his head. Dane's fingers splayed over her back as he held onto her as if he thought she might slip away. He deepened the kiss, loving the taste of wine and chocolate soufflé from the dessert they'd shared.

Before Dane could think of whether he should stop himself or not, he was cupping her ass, pressing her against the erection that had grown quickly. She moved her hips, pumping against him and Dane thought if he were a lion this would be the part where he roared, loud and strong. With one hand he gathered the material of her skirt until he felt the smooth skin of her thigh and then the bare curve of her ass. Whatever she wore by way of underwear didn't cover her completely and the thought had him aching inside.

On a hungry moan, Zera lifted her leg, wrapping it around his waist. Dane had missed this, the instant lick of wantonness that came when Zera was officially aroused. It was like flicking on a light switch and being offered a view into the erotic desires of a beautiful black goddess. It surpassed any dream or image, engulfing him with a certainty that he would never experience this again.

Dane lifted her other leg, locking them both behind his back as his tongue continued to duel with hers. He walked them back to the bench where she'd previously sat. He turned, sitting down and holding her on his lap, his hands coming up, fingers delving into her mass of hair to scrape lightly along her scalp. Her hands came down to his shoulders, kneading and then gripping the material of his shirt. The kiss grew hungrier, more desperate as his heart rapped mercilessly against his ribs. Her legs stayed tightly around him, her center pressing against his groin as if they were totally naked.

He groaned raggedly, his teeth scraping over the line of her jaw as their mouths finally parted. She moaned and gyrated over him. Dane let his hands fall down to her back, holding her as she arched over him. He lowered his face until he could brush a cheek over her breast. The breathy sound she made in response made him want to call out her name. He rubbed his face over her other breast, then covered one nipple with his open mouth. He didn't care that she still wore her shirt and bra. It didn't matter that they were on the deck of a yacht he'd rented for the evening. Nothing mattered but the feel of her in his arms, the sound of her voice in his ear. Nothing mattered at all.

"I can't."

Dane went instantly still at the sound of those two words. They seemed to quietly fall over the heat that had shrouded him, but landed like a deafening blow. On the inside he still burned for her. On the outside, he slowly lifted his head to stare at her.

She was still on top of him, but sitting up straight now, her gaze intent as she stared at him.

"I am not willing to have another affair with you, Dane," she said evenly. "I simply cannot afford to go down that road again."

Before he could find any words, Zera moved off of him. She stood in front of him for a moment waiting for his comment, but when it did not come, she turned away. He watched her go to where her shoes were sitting by a table and two chairs. She sat in one of the chairs and put each shoe on her foot, tying the straps around her ankles and then pushing her skirt down.

"You have to understand," she began when he still hadn't spoken.

Dane stood and cleared his throat. "I do," he told her, cutting off whatever else she may have wanted to say. "I understand completely and I will respect your wishes. It is getting late. I'll instruct the captain to take us back now."

CHAPTER 5

Zera knew now without any doubt, that she was out of her mind. Her body would certainly agree, as twenty minutes later the hum of unsatisfied arousal still buzzed throughout her every pore.

She walked with quick strides down the street. Dane was right beside her. He'd insisted on walking her back to her car. She hadn't realized they would do so in complete silence. Was he angry because she'd stopped their little interlude on the yacht? Did he really want to have another affair with her that badly? Settling down with one woman was not in Dane's future. He'd told her that the night they'd first met the last time he was in Paris. She'd been fine with hearing that because she wasn't looking to get involved in anything serious either. Truth be told, Zera hadn't come to Paris for any of the romance included in the city's reputation.

"Your phone's ringing."

"Huh?" Zera asked when Dane's hand touched her shoulder.

"Your phone," he said, pointing down at the small purse she was carrying. "It's ringing."

"Oh!" Zera reached down and into the purse. She pulled out her phone and hurriedly answered without looking at the screen.

"He's dead," the familiar male voice on the other end announced.

"What?" she replied and stopped herself from asking who was dead.

They were still about half a block away from the car park and she knew that telling Dane she could go the rest of the way on her own was pointless.

"Debare's body was found in a hotel room late last night. We just got word and I thought you should know."

Zera swallowed and did her best to keep walking when her legs had suddenly turned wobbly. "Yeah. Ah, thanks for letting me know," she managed. She had more questions but knew she couldn't go into them right now.

"You can come home now," he said. "Or at least back to Arlington, I mean."

"No," she replied instantly. "I can't. Not yet."

"Zera?"

"Look, I'm gonna have to call you back. I'm about to get in my car and drive and you know what a hazard it is to talk on a cell phone while driving. I'll catch up with you later."

She disconnected the call before anymore could be said. Words were the last thing she needed right now. Zera needed to think. This was unexpected and it was problematic and she had to figure out what her next steps would be and…

"Is something wrong?"

Her head snapped to the side as she came to an abrupt stop. Dane was still beside her.

"Ah, no. Nothing is wrong." She lied. "Just an old friend from home."

Dane stood on the sidewalk with the city's picture-perfect backdrop behind him. The cobblestone path of the left bank was just below the street where they now walked, so the sounds of the river and the lights from the Pont Neuf were still present.

"That friend told you something that surprised you," he said. "That friend upset you."

"No," she replied shaking her head a little too adamantly. "Nothing like that. I'm good. Just a little tired. Want to hurry and get home."

His gaze narrowed, but he did not respond. He continued walking. Zera followed. Still holding her phone in one hand she dug into her purse with the other and pulled out her car keys.

"I'm just up on the second level," she said when they came to the double door entrance of the car park. "You don't have to go up with me."

He paused again and looked as if he wanted to say something. Maybe he wanted to ask her more questions. If she were in his position she'd wonder herself what was going on. But Zera was not in Dane's position. She was still in the spot she'd been in for almost five years now. This was still her priority over any and everything else.

"I'll call you tomorrow," she said. She desperately wanted to do and say more, but couldn't. Zera leaned in to place a quick kiss on Dane's lips before heading into the car park.

He had looked as if he wanted to insist on going to her car with her, but Zera had moved fast not to allow him that choice.

As she walked up the flight of stairs and turned down the numbered aisle where she'd parked her car, Zera half expected to see a white rose on her windshield. That was how Aasir normally reached out to her, as direct contact was dangerous for both of them. But the news of Debare's murder was big. Hence the reason Aasir had just called her instead. After finding the white rose in her apartment three nights ago, Zera had already traveled to their meeting spot and had spoken to Aasir. Now, it seems the tentative plan they'd put in place during that call would be changed.

There was no rose on her car, but she slipped behind the wheel and closed the door. Dropping her purse on the passenger seat, she reached into the glove compartment and pulled out her Bluetooth. When it was attached to her phone and she'd started the car's engine, Zera found the number stored in her phone's memory and dialed it.

"We have a problem," was the first thing she said when the woman on the other end answered.

"I know," she replied. "Get to a safe place and we'll figure out what to do about it."

Dane didn't care what was going on with Zera.

He really didn't.

He'd resigned himself to the fact that they were still attracted to each other and he was willing to act on that. With eleven days left in his two-week trip, he had other things to do with his time, if sleeping with Zera again wasn't an option. What he was not going to do was spend any of that time wondering why she looked so damn spooked when she received that call.

It was none of his business. Who she had been speaking to and whatever they'd said to her had nothing to do with Dane. So he should simply let it go. But an hour after leaving her, he was still sitting at the small desk in his hotel room, staring at his laptop screen. He'd googled her and read as much information available online, which wasn't much. Aside from her name, a Facebook page that she hadn't visited in three years, and a picture of her when she was seventeen and had been awarded two full scholarships as well as an international grant which Dane had never even heard of before, were all he could find.

She'd attended college in the United States, something else Dane had not known. Tuskegee University was where she'd studied political science, or at least that's what she'd stated were her plans when she was interviewed after receiving that large endowment. The name of the foundation that had funded the grant seemed vaguely familiar to Dane and for the next hour he found himself deeply entrenched in a rabbit hole studying the Fordhiem Reitz Foundation.

When Dane glanced at the clock to see that it was nearing three in the morning, he shut down the laptop and moved to the bed. He checked his phone which had been connected to the charger on the nightstand and noted no text messages. Dane held the phone for another couple of seconds before opening a new message screen and typing:

CAN'T STOP THINKING OF YOU

He stared at those words wondering if he should send the text, or delete it and go to bed. As an unstated rule Dane did not do overly personal or emotional text messages. For him, text messages served a purpose of quick communication of important facts, times, appointment changes, etc. The people he dealt with on a personal level, he either talked to in person or on the phone.

Dane was tired and it was late. He sent the message, switched off the lamp on the nightstand and lay down in the bed. He'd pushed the duvet and sheet back when he'd first entered the room, and now pulled them to cover his body. He closed his eyes even though he knew sleep would not come quickly. This had been the routine for the last three days. This was his time to think about Zera without the guilt of needing to focus on either his supposed relaxation or the business endeavor.

Tonight he'd touched her skin, felt the curve of her ass and just a brief hint of the heat burning between her legs. She'd straddled him and memories of her riding him until his release had almost paralyzed him were vivid in his mind. His dick hardened at the thoughts, but Dane's breathing remained normal. He could think about her, be aroused by her, and not lose his control. For Dane, control was so much more than a virtue. It was a life-line. Throughout all that had happened to him in these past couple of years, he hadn't lost control. He hadn't lashed out at any of the Donovan cousins that had looked at him with disdain, or the ones who had insulted his mother. He hadn't even pulled the trigger to end his mother's life when he knew that was what needed to happen to keep more people safe.

What he did do was lick his lips as he recalled his tongue tracing a path down Zera's neck and dancing over her covered nipple. He wanted to taste her skin-to-skin. Every inch of her, one more time. He wanted to… His phone chimed.

LIKEWISE. BUT THERE IS NO POINT.

After reaching over for the phone and reading her message, Dane fell back against his pillow.

PLEASURE IS A VALID POINT

INDEED IT IS, was her response.

And just like that Dane wished he could see her again.

SEND ME A PICTURE TO GO WITH MY THOUGHTS

This was way beyond Dane keeping personal out of his text

messages. It was, in fact, something he'd never imagined himself doing. Hadn't there been a slew of celebrities and politicians whose phones had been hacked and personal pictures plastered all over the Internet? This message, and whatever response she might send, was not smart. Still, he waited with bated breath for her response.

There was a long pause and for a minute he'd thought she wouldn't send it. No, he'd actually thought he was a fool for requesting it. An immature fool who was letting his hormones get the best of him.

But then her response came in the form of a picture.

He felt like a kid on Christmas morning, his thumb actually shaking as he pressed the button to open the picture.

YOUR HANDS FELT LIKE HEAVEN LAST NIGHT

And she was heaven-sent. If there were hot as sin African women lying naked in a bed in heaven. Her face wasn't in the photo and it really only showed her leg, all the way up to her hip, gloriously bare. But apparently that was enough for his attention-starved libido.

The hard-on which had been slowly growing before this exchange, began to now throb painfully. He could end this ridiculously self-imposed torture. Stop texting her and attempt to go to sleep with a hard dick and his relief probably miles away. He could force himself to stop thinking about Zera and to not let her invade his life the way she had the first time. He could do it. He'd walked away and left her in his past before. There was no reason why he couldn't do it again. Except that this physical need for her was too potent to ignore and because what he wanted more than the control he was famous for, was the pleasure he knew would only come from her.

I WANT TO TOUCH YOU AGAIN. ALL OF YOU.

Once more she took a while to respond.

I'VE MISSED YOU.

He ached for her.

I CAN BE THERE IN MINUTES. GIVE ME YOUR ADDRESS.

NO.

That response had come immediately and Dane frowned. What the hell was going on with her?

IS THERE SOMEONE ELSE?

His fingers had moved stiffly as he'd typed that question.

NO

Another quick reply.

THEN WHY?

Dane waited for her response but it never came and when he woke the next morning it was with a curse on his lips. Not only did he still have an amazingly irritating erection, but now his phone battery was also dead.

At close to six o'clock in the evening, Zera sat on a bench in the garden of Musée Zadkine. With one leg crossed over the other, her gray Eddie Bauer backpack close to her right hip, and the barely used iPad on her lap, she waited for the incoming Skype call.

It was so peaceful here, cuddled between immaculately manicured lawns and shrubbery, and the stark distinct flare of sculptures by the Russian born, Ossip Zadkine. Zadkine had once lived in the house behind where Zera now sat. He'd also worked there and upon his death the place was turned into a museum. One of the many in the 6th Arrondissement that Zera had frequented since Emmet's death.

When she awakened yesterday morning, it was to a persistent knocking on her door by Ines, an up and coming model who lived on the lower level of Zera's apartment building.

"You get deliveries from suitors early in the morning. I am jealous."

Ines was just an inch or so shorter than Zera. French-born, with long brown hair and expression-filled brown eyes, Ines was a European beauty that was about to take over the fashion industry.

Zera had taken the long-stemmed white rose from Ines, running her fingers over the dethorned stem as she thought about what it meant.

"Not at all," Zera had replied. "I am still as single as you are."

"But someone is interested," Ines replied as she turned to leave. "That is more than I have right now."

Ines had begun singing as she traveled down the hall and then the stairs. It was a Cardi B song that Zera detested, so she yelled "thanks" and quickly closed her door.

With the message received, Zera was now in the secluded spot of her choice, awaiting Aasir's Skype call which always came at 6pm the evening following the day she received the rose. Aasir only used disposable cell phones whenever he called her directly. And when they met via Skype, which she was hoping to do now, she used an iPad that was registered to Ines's grandmother.

Zera tapped her fingers on the screen of the iPad. Her cell phone was in her pocket and she'd turned up the volume on the ringtone, just in case. It was very quiet here at this time of evening, so she didn't have to worry about not hearing the call. Especially if no call came through.

With a heavy sigh she closed her eyes and tried once again to remain calm. The past couple of nights she'd been restless and not just because of the news of Debare's death—although that was going to change the course of so many things on the horizon. Dane's text messages had aroused and confused her. How was she supposed to do this again? She could not resist him. She'd tried really hard last night and to an extent she supposed she'd won, but Zera knew that would be short-lived.

There was no doubt that she wanted him, and he apparently wanted her. But what would happen after they satisfied that need? Where would that lead them? To more lies, Zera thought. She'd always be lying to him, just as she had before. There was no other option, and Zera hated that fact. She hated that to do what she knew she was meant to do, she had to give up what a part of her recognized as something very special.

Her cell phone rang loud enough to wake the dead and Zera jumped before pulling it out of her pocket to answer. She checked the screen and saw with immediate disappointment that it was not Aasir.

"Hi Ines," she answered.

The willowy thin woman with the husky voice, answered in her deep French-accented voice.

"Hello, Zera. Where are you?" she asked.

"I'm running some errands," was Zera's quick response.

"We were going to have dinner. Did you forget?"

Zera had forgotten.

"Sorry, I meant to call you to cancel. Have to get some things done," Zera told her.

"That is okay. Also, I told the guy that stopped by looking for you that you would possibly be back in an hour. Guess that will be a bit longer now. He said he would not mind the wait."

Zera froze at Ines's words.

"What guy?"

"He was here just a few moments ago. That is why I thought to call you to remind you about dinner and tell you that he was here."

The iPad almost slipped from Zera's lap as she uncrossed her legs and sat up straighter on the bench.

"Who was it? Did he leave a name or contact information?" she asked.

"No name. Just dark glasses and a frown when I said you were not here. He did smell good," Ines said.

Zera was much more concerned with who would show up at her apartment looking for her when nobody was supposed to know where she was. She quickly stuffed the iPad into her back pack and closed it.

"If he comes back, ask questions Ines," Zera instructed.

"Fine. When do you think you will return?"

That was a good question. Zera didn't plan to return. Not now.

"I will call you back. Remember, ask questions if he returns."

"Should I send you a text message?"

"No!" Zera replied and then sighed as she realized she'd practically yelled at Ines. "I mean, no that won't be necessary. I will call you back but it may be from a different number, so just answer all calls tonight."

"Are you kidding? I always answer all calls. Never know when the one that will have me on a jet heading to another, better paying photo shoot might come."

Ines was getting job after job, but she had yet to hit the big runways for the famous Fashion Weeks. Zera knew that they were coming for her even if Ines was a bit impatient.

"Right. Okay. I have to go. Answer your phone," Zera instructed.

She disconnected the call. She put the iPad in her pack and slipped the strap of the backpack onto her shoulder before she stood. Her steps were halted by a noise. Zera looked around the garden. The sculptures that she'd once looked at with interest, now seemed creepy—their tall elongated forms casting shadows over an area that she hadn't seen before. She immediately turned and headed back inside through the French doors of the museum. Today she was wearing leggings and an old denim shirt and tank top, tennis shoes and a black baseball cap. Pulling the cap down further on her head, she moved fast, thoughts of getting back to her car foremost in her mind.

Once she was out of the museum and on the sidewalk, Zera tried to blend in with a crowd of people that were coming up behind her, but before she could, she spotted him. He was across the street, leaning against a dark gray car, legs crossed at the ankles, dark sunglasses covering his eyes. Zera didn't know how she knew it was him, and she didn't know exactly who he was, but her steps hastened. The car park was farther than she'd liked to consider as she moved through the people on the sidewalk, while looking over her shoulder.

He was no longer leaning on the car.

She cursed and started to run. Her phone was in her hand, all she had to do was make a call and all of this would stop. She would be safe and this would be over, finally. But Hiari would still be missing. Zera kept running. She came to the car park and pushed through the door, taking the stairs two at a time to the level she was on. Zera heard the screech of tires the minute she turned down the aisle where her car was parked. She moved as fast as she could, but the car was coming, headlights blaring through the dim area. Turning quickly she knelt by the passenger side door and used her key to unlock it. The car was turning around. Zera climbed into her car, moving over the console to get into the driver's seat. With shaking hands she managed to start the ignition and backed out just as the other car had turned and floored the gas. He was going to run right into her. The impact might not kill her but would definitely cause a great deal of damage to her and the car. She turned the steering wheel and stepped on the gas. Her car whirled around and she drove out of the car park with the other car right behind her.

Paris traffic was no playground, but Zera had been mastering it for years now, so she managed to get at least six cars ahead of the dark sedan that was after her now. She weaved in and out of traffic, going against all the rules of the road until she could turn down one street and then another and another. Twenty minutes and what seemed like half her lifetime later, Zera glanced in her rearview mirror and almost sighed with relief when she no longer saw the car.

But she didn't stop driving and she didn't dare circle back to return to her apartment. They never worked solo. So whoever had knocked on the door to her apartment building was probably still there waiting for her return. These two, because she knew there were two—the one who had been so casually leaning against the gray car, and the one who had already been waiting for her at the car park—would not stop looking for her either. If they were sent for her, not following through on that order wasn't an option. Unsuccessful assignments most often lead to painful deaths.

Zera knew that rule all too well.

She drove fast, her heart thumping as she tried to think of what her next step would be. She couldn't call anyone, couldn't go back. Not now. So instead, she went forward, to the only place she'd ever been able to find comfort.

CHAPTER 6

*D*ane sat on the couch in the suite at the Hôtel San Régis where his first face-to-face meeting with Roark, Ridge and Suri Donovan was taking place.

This hotel was an obvious upgrade from where he was staying, but Dane had purposely selected his hotel. He hadn't wanted any extra attention during this trip and it was close to two of his favorite sights to see in Paris—the Eiffel Tower and the Seine. As his trip was to be a bit of pleasure combined with business, Dane was aiming for comfort. The San Régis was a five-star hotel that specialized in discretion. Roark had advised Dane via email that he'd reserved two suites for all of the meetings they had scheduled.

"It's nice to finally meet you in person," Suri said after the four of them had sat in silence for the first ten minutes after Dane entered the room.

"Likewise," Dane replied with a nod in her direction.

She was twenty-eight years old. At five feet tall, she was

clearly the shortest of all the Donovans in the room. Her hair was an array of curls clustered to one side beneath a short brimmed black hat. She wore a black and white striped jacket and form-fitting black pants with high-heeled black boots. Her lipstick was bright red and her brown eyes were full of laughter. She was a recent graduate from Cambridge where she'd studied art history and economics.

Dane had done his homework on all of the Donovan family members.

"We've heard a lot about you," she continued with a heavy British accent.

"I can imagine," Dane replied. He did not imagine that everything they'd heard about him was complimentary.

Suri chuckled. "It was not all bad. Actually, Bailey speaks highly of you. And I can tell you that means something because Bailey can be quite hard to impress."

"You're right about that," Ridge added with a shake of his head.

Ridge was the middle child. His complexion the same chocolate-brown hue as his sister's. He wore a low-cut neatly trimmed beard like his brother, but also had black dreadlocks that were twisted in some fashion at the top and held together with a band at the nape of his neck to hang down his back. He was dressed in dark gray slacks, a royal blue shirt and matching gray vest. Ridge was also a graduate of Cambridge where he'd studied law.

"We know everything that happened back in the States," Ridge continued. "And for the record we think you got a shabby deal. Your parents did you wrong from the start but we do not get to choose them, now do we?"

"No," Dane replied as he considered those words. "I guess we don't."

He was beginning to think he might like these newfound cousins.

"What matters is that we are family and that we have some new business to tend to," Roark, the oldest of these Donovan children interjected.

This one was everything Bernard had told Dane he would be and a little more. As the oldest child of Gabriel and Maxine Donovan, Roark had just turned thirty-eight last month. That made him two years younger than Dane, who had a birthday coming later this year. Roark stood six feet even, one inch shorter than Ridge. His complexion was much lighter than his siblings, the hair on his head and beard jet black. He wore a navy blue suit, of which the jacket lay neatly over the arm of the chair where he sat across from Dane.

"A focus on clean energy is a great idea. It is a new and upcoming market and we are prime to make our already lucrative companies, even stronger, from this venture," Roark said.

Dane nodded, ready to get down to business. "I agree. Now, there are just a few details that we need to iron out before we begin with the interviews."

At those words, Dane reached into his briefcase which he'd set on the floor beside him when he took his seat, and grabbed the folders he'd prepared before he left the States. He gave each one of his cousins a folder and their meeting officially began.

It was four hours, dinner, drinks, and an invitation to London to meet his Aunt Maxine, later, when Dane finally arrived back at his hotel. Roark was returning to London tonight because he had more meetings at the office in the morning, but Suri and Ridge were going to stay in the reserved suites at the San Régis. They'd invited Dane to lunch tomorrow and instead of immediately declining, he'd told them he would call them in the morning. He supposed, for them, it seemed normal to have lunch with their cousin. Perhaps it was more like a family reunion for them since they were the only part of the Donovan family that did not live in the U.S. For Dane, the casual connection wasn't normal at all.

Dane's family life had been a little different from what he suspected the rest of the Donovans had experienced. His mother, Roslyn, had a personality disorder but had managed to raise Dane and his sister Jaydon, in a loving home. She sent them to private schools and made sure they had everything they needed, all between mini-mental breaks where she would rage, scream and lock herself in her bedroom for days at a time. As Dane had gone through the things in Roslyn's New York apartment, he'd found a box of her private papers. Among the papers were unfilled prescriptions for an anti-psychotic drug and two versions of Dane's birth certificate. One which named him Dane Henry Ausby and the other, Dane Henry Donovan. From the time he was five years old his mother had told him that he was a Donovan. The DNA test that Bernard had taken last year finally proved Roslyn's claim. It had taken Dane weeks to ensure that his correct birth certificate was now the only one on record.

Dane doubted very seriously that Roark, Ridge or Suri, or any of his other cousins, had to deal with a situation like that. So yeah, his idea of family was very different from theirs.

Now, Dane stepped off the elevator and walked down the hall to his room. It was just after nine in the evening. He wondered what Zera was doing. This time two nights ago, she'd been in his arms as they sailed along the Seine. A part of him wanted her in his arms again, while the other—perhaps, smarter —part thought he should definitely steer clear of Zera on this trip. The alarmed look on her face the other night after she'd taken that call should have been enough to convince him that there was a lot about the woman that he just did not want to know. Like her connection to Emmet Parks. Shaking his head, Dane reached into his jacket pocket for the key to unlock his door.

He was definitely going to stay away from Zera. He didn't have time for whatever games she was most likely still playing. Dane opened the door. He stepped inside and frowned. Something was wrong. He knew it the moment the door closed with a loud thud behind him.

"I wanted to see you," Zera said and licked her lips. "I couldn't stop thinking about our last conversation."

Dane stared at her, trying to keep the magnitude of the shock at seeing her sitting in the chair near the window of his hotel room, to himself.

He moved slowly, setting his briefcase down near the round table and additional chairs. "How did you get in here?" he asked.

"Money is always a proper motivator," she replied.

"So you bribed someone for a key to my room," he said. "After you hacked into all the hotels in the area to find out where I was staying."

During their dinner on the yacht, Zera had finally admitted that was how she'd located him. Dane had been surprised and intrigued. He'd never really given much thought to what her profession was when he'd first met her. At this point, he wondered how else she was using the unique skillset of being a hacker.

"Yes and yes," she answered, this time with a shrug. "I guess that means you're one hell of a lover. If a woman's willing to go through all that trouble to find you."

Dane wasn't the type to brag about his prowess, even if he did know how to keep a woman pleasured. He recalled that each time he had been with Zera she'd been pleased. They both had been. He also recognized a brush-off when he heard one.

She stood from the chair and walked toward where Dane was still seemingly rooted to the spot by the table.

"During our text exchange you said you couldn't stop thinking about me," she said, her voice lower, huskier.

She wore leggings that sculpted her long, lean legs. A white tank top that was equally as tight, was covered by a shirt that she'd left unbuttoned. The polka dot tennis shoes she'd worn the night he'd seen her at the museum added a touch of whimsy to the otherwise sexy as hell outfit. Dane's fingers clenched at his side as he anticipated the moment he would finally get his hands on her.

"If you don't recall, I saved the text messages," she finished when she was standing directly in front of him.

Dane removed his suit jacket and loosened the tie at his neck.

"Hunting me down and saving my text messages," he said. "I guess I should be flattered."

She reached up and finished undoing his tie, slipping it from his neck with a slow and seductive motion.

"No," she whispered, her fingers going to the top buttons of his shirt. "You should be ready."

Zera stood even closer to him now, so close that her breasts brushed against his chest. Dane kept his arms at his sides, even when she had completely unbuttoned his shirt and pulled it down his arms, letting it drop to the floor. He did not move when she lifted the undershirt he wore up and over his head, dropping it so that it joined the other garment on the floor. When her palms flattened on his bare chest heat soared throughout his body, pooling in the already pronounced throbbing of his dick.

Dane closed his eyes when she leaned down to drop soft kisses over his pectoral muscles. He let himself think back to all the times she'd put her mouth on him in the past. Damn, he really enjoyed her mouth. It was such a talented and uninhibited mouth. He could easily let her continue to do whatever she wanted with it because he was fairly certain he knew how it would end. But as Zera begin to kiss lower down his abs, her hands touching his arms lightly as she moved, Dane opened his eyes. He wrapped his fingers around her wrists and took a step back away from her. When she looked up at him in surprise, her lips parted, tongue peeking between the rows of perfectly white teeth, he almost groaned with regret.

"The other night you said you did not want to be part of another affair," he told her because he needed to be sure. *She* needed to be sure. From this point on there was no going back and Dane prided himself on never doing anything a woman didn't want to do. He did not do mixed signals or miscommunication. She was either all in for this interlude, or all out. There was no middle ground.

"And tonight you're here, doing this," he continued, his words now coming through clenched teeth.

She licked her lips and Dane's dick pressed painfully against the zipper of his pants.

"I'm where I want to be, doing what I want to do," she stated.

For a few silent seconds their gazes held, but they did not move.

Then Dane released her wrists. He undid the buckle of his belt and the button of his slacks, before pushing the zipper down. She swatted his hands out of the way at that point, pushing his pants down his legs before rubbing her cheek over the bulge of his dick still covered by his boxers. As if knowing it was being summoned, his dick poked through the slit of his boxers and Zera sighed, before breathing over the turgid crest. She quickly pushed the boxers down to his knees, before wrapping her long fingers around the base of his cock. Dane thrust his fingers into her hair, pushing through the thick mass until the band that had been holding it back in a ponytail snapped free. He buried his hands in the dark tresses and braced himself for the jolt of pleasure he knew was coming the moment her mouth closed over the head of his cock. But she didn't take him that way, not just yet.

Instead she stroked him from the base to the tip, holding him tight. The warmth of her palms and the feel of her breath whispering over his length had Dane clenching his teeth to the point in which he thought he might actually crack one from the pressure. He wanted to toss his head back, close his eyes and moan with the anticipation of release, but instead he watched her. Her lids were lowered as she stared down at his shaft as if memorizing its shape, length, and feel. And when a drop of pre-cum appeared at the tip, her perfect tongue snaked out to swipe it away. His fingers tightened in her hair and her name tumbled from his lips.

She looked up at him then, triumph clear in her gaze. He

wanted to warn her to stop toying with him, but he refrained. His turn would come soon and he would make her pay. For now, he'd let his little uninhibited vixen have her fun.

Zera loved the feel of his hands in her hair, even when he wrapped the strands around his hand and tugged so that her scalp stung just a bit. The quick jolt of pain heightened the pleasure of feeling his thick length between her lips. She held him steady, her palms damp from the saliva that now coated his dick. The way he slipped inside her mouth, pushed back to touch her throat, then slid out once more had her pussy pulsating and her nipples tingling. She relaxed her throat muscles in time for his next thrust and tilted her head back slightly. He moved in deeper as her tongue glided slowly against the underside of his dick.

Dane groaned and Zera continued to work his dick in and out of her mouth. She knew he loved this. She recalled how he used to get off by watching her through partially closed eyes as she gave him a blow job. He'd told her once that he'd never seen anyone as sexy as her. The words, the memories, all of it had stuck with her through the many nights she'd spent alone since then. And she missed it. She missed him.

His fingers left her hair to slide down to her face. His thumbs brushed over her cheeks and then down to her lips that were still wrapped around his dick. With one hand he grabbed himself, slipping his thickness out of her mouth. Zera kept her lips firm so that their connection broke with a popping sound. He rubbed the moist tip over her chin, then along the line of her jaw, telling her to "Look at me," while he did. She looked at him, falling deep into his dark gaze the same way she had before. His lips were parted so that she could see his teeth. His eyes were open wide now, the muscles in his chest bulging so that he appeared like a dark god standing before her.

"Did you miss this?" Dane asked while moving his engorged dick over one cheek and then the other.

The warmth of his skin against hers caused Zera to shiver. Her lips trembled as she responded, "Yes."

"Tell me," he insisted, this time tapping his length over her lips while he waited for her to respond.

Zera swallowed. She wanted to lick him again, to take him deep and suck hard. Instead, she opened her mouth and breathed over the tip of his dick before whispering, "I missed this."

Her tongue snaked out at that point, licking yet another drop of pre-cum. She savored the taste, closed her eyes and moaned.

Dane moved back at that moment. He bent over and tucked his hands beneath her arms, bringing them both to a standing position. He held her gaze as he removed the shirt and the tank top she wore beneath it up and over her head. His hands were warm as they reached around to her back and unhooked her bra. Zera simply did not move. She let the bra slide down her arms and fall to the floor. Her breasts felt heavy and ached for him to touch them, but Dane's gaze never faltered from hers.

His hands moved down to the ban of her leggings. He pushed them down past her hips, his crafty fingers hooking the thin strap of the thong she wore and dragging them down as well. He moved down like her clothes, keeping his head tilted so that he could continue to stare up into her eyes, until his face was just a breath away from her mound. Her legs shook as he untied her tennis shoes and lifted one leg, then the next to remove them, her leggings and the thong. When he was finished and she thought he would look away from her and at least drop a moist kiss on her now throbbing center, he did not.

Dane stayed down, removing his own shoes, socks and then standing to push his pants and boxer briefs down and off. He was naked and so was she, but Zera had no clue what to do next. Should she step closer to him? Maybe take his dick in her hand and guide him to where she desperately needed it to be? Should she push him back to the couch and straddle him as she'd done while they were fully dressed on the yacht? Or…

He picked her up. With one arm around her waist, Dane lifted her off the floor. Zera's hands instantly went to his chest, her breathing coming in quick pants. He was going to carry her to the bed, lay her down and drive into her hard and fast. Yes! That's exactly what she needed to work off the adrenaline that still pulsed through her veins. And to clear her mind of all the thoughts that were running through it as a result of the adrenaline rush.

She was startled when he only took a couple steps and her butt met the cool surface of the table as he set her there. He put a hand to her cheek and tilted her head back seconds before his lips crashed down over hers. His mouth moved hungrily over hers and Zera struggled to keep up. He was pushing her back while they kissed, until she lay flat on the dark wood-colored table. Ending the kiss, Dane sucked her bottom lip into his mouth and Zera dug her nails into the skin on his shoulders. When he released her she was breathless. She propped herself up on her elbows as he moved lower, flicking his tongue over her taut nipples. Zera's head fell back at the connection and she clenched her teeth in anticipation. But Dane did not suck her breasts the way she wanted him to, the way she'd remembered him doing so masterfully before.

He moved lower. His hands splayed over her, easing slowly down her torso. A finger circled her navel and another traced the outline of her mound. Zera's whole body trembled as he bent down, this time lifting her legs to drop one over each shoulder. She had only seconds to grasp the edge of the table and hold on before his fingers parted her now moist folds and his mouth suckled greedily on her clit. Her back arched and her toes curled, sound dying in her throat, as he continued the delicious torture. When her thighs would not stop shaking no matter how much she willed them to do so, Dane placed his palms on both thighs and moved from her clit to lick up and down her center.

Zera felt like screaming out in pleasure, or possibly spontaneously combusting at the pent-up passion that had lay dormant for far too long. He pressed two fingers inside of her and Zera bit her bottom lip. He pulled those fingers out and she cursed.

"Look at me!" he commanded.

She lifted her head so that she could stare down at him. His lips were glossed with her essence, beads of her moisture clung to his mustache and the chin portion of his beard. He dipped his head again, this time pressing his tongue into the opening his fingers had just vacated. She moaned long and loud before her hips lifted from the table to pump against his mouth.

Zera wanted to close her eyes to the ecstasy, but she dare not. She wanted to yell at him to just hurry up and fuck her for goodness' sake! But she did not. That's not how it worked with Dane. He always wanted more, to push further, go the extra mile, every time. She had to prove that she could go the distance with him, every time. So she continued to pump and he continued to thrust his tongue in and out of her, but when a finger lightly brushed her anus she lost the battle. Her climax came fast and hard, her guttural moan was deep and loud. His satisfied groan as he continued to lick every bit of her release was her reward.

But Dane was not finished.

Zera had no idea when he'd retrieved a condom, but she heard the tearing of the packet and managed to see through her sated haze in time to watch him smoothing the latex over his thick erection. Before she could blink, he was inside of her, buried to the hilt, and holding still as if waiting for her to acclimate herself to his presence. That wasn't easy. He filled her and not just physically. From the moment he'd walked into this room she'd felt him, snaking into her life and winding himself completely around her so that she could only think of coming to him when she'd needed a place to go. This was her shelter, Zera thought as her muscles tightened around his length. He whispered her name and she lifted her gaze to meet his. It was there in the darkness of his eyes, the clenching of his jaw and the sheer strength of his physique. He was her safe haven when she never thought she needed one.

Dane began moving slowly, a dance that was familiar and yet this moment seemed totally new. He circled his hips, pressing into her from different angles before thrusting so fast her breasts jiggled and she had to hold on to keep from sliding completely off the table. That was the best, the force, his length, his girth, him. Just him.

Her second release was quick and fast soaring through her like a burst of fireworks.

"Yes," Dane whispered as her body tensed and her release seeped out of her.

He did not stop moving inside of her, not until minutes later when his own release claimed him. He tensed over her, his fingers digging into the skin of her thighs as he turned his face so that the scrape of his beard and his lips brushed over her ankle.

Time stood still, but then it didn't. Zera knew the moment Dane recovered from his release because something slipped away from her. It wasn't something physical, but a feeling, a presence, just left. She looked at him and watched as he moved his hips to pull out of her. He put her legs down slowly and stepped back to stare down at her.

She figured she must look strange laying on top of a table where he'd maybe had a meal at some point. But then, she hadn't been the one to select this location for their tryst. Zera pushed herself up until she was sitting on the table, her legs dangling from the sides. She wanted to say something clever, or at least cordial, but she didn't know what.

Dane extended a hand to her and said, "Come on. Let's get a shower."

So words weren't necessary. She was good with that for the moment because she really did not know how she was going to explain her "not another affair" status from just two nights ago, to "yeah, I'll let you fuck me on your table" just a few moments ago. Silence was good. She had things to think about anyway, so if Dane just wanted to crash after their shower, she wasn't going to argue.

Forty minutes later they lay in the bed, lights out. Zera allowed herself to relax in Dane's arms, to close her eyes and not feel the intense fear she'd felt when she'd been running for her life. Things had gotten very serious, very fast and she had to figure out what her next step was. But damn she was tired. She had to sleep first.

Zera had just closed her eyes and settled into Dane's warmth, when he said, "Now you can tell me why you really paid someone to let you into my room."

CHAPTER 7

*D*ane frowned as he once again checked email on his phone. He'd been doing this multiple times a day for the past week. The message he was looking for had not come through. Which meant the questions he had still went unanswered.

Slipping his phone back into his front pant pocket, Dane put the car in drive and pulled out of the parking spot. After about a mile, he was stopped in traffic and he drummed his fingers over the steering wheel, his mind circling back to the call he'd been forced to make a week ago.

Dane had been standing on the balcony at the hotel the morning after sleeping with Zera again.

"Hi. It's Dane. I need you to do something for me. You can invoice me and I'll pay you, but I don't want this on the books with D&D Investigations."

D&D Investigations was a private investigation firm which was started by Dane's ex-Navy SEAL cousin, Trent Donovan and former homicide detective, Sam Desdune. There are two locations for the company, one in Los Angeles where Trent, his wife, Tia and their son Trevor live. And the other is in Greenwich, Connecticut where the Desdune family, and now Bailey and Devlin live.

"Whoa there. Let's start with, hi Bailey, how are you today?"

He'd held the phone to his ear with one hand and ran a hand down the back of his head with the other.

"Hi, Bailey. How's married life treating you?" he asked, his voice just a little more restrained than it had been when she'd first answered her phone.

"It's an adjustment," she replied. "But I'm still up for the challenge. Besides, it's been nine months and we haven't killed each other yet. So I'm counting that as progress."

She chuckled and Dane couldn't help but join in. Bailey was married to Trent's best friend and Navy SEAL Devlin Bonner, the man who killed Dane's mother. Even thinking about that now it seemed odd to not want to break Dev's neck in retaliation. But the circumstances that night at the Karing for Kidz Foundation's annual fundraiser had been extreme. And if Dev hadn't taken the shot, Dane would have been forced to. Later, Dev had told Dane he'd done him a favor so that Dane would not have to carry the guilt of killing his own mother. Dane had to be grateful to the guy for that.

"That's a good thing," Dane replied. "And no baby on the way yet, I presume."

"Oh no! You will not join in that party, Dane Donovan," Bailey said. "Dad, Brandon and even Brock, are on what they call the 'Bailey Baby Watch'. It's insane."

She was probably right, but it was cute. To have a family who loved that much and wished only for happiness, prosperity and pro-creation, was a blessing. Right?

"I'm just kidding," Dane said with a smile. "Brynne says Bernard is riding her about giving him another grandchild since Keysa's already given him Madison Lee."

"Still not ready to call him "dad", huh?" Bailey asked, her tone just a little more serious this time. "It's okay. I understand. It's a big adjustment after all that happened."

Dane had folded one arm over his chest. He was looking out to the clear morning sky, inhaling deeply and exhaling slowly.

"It is an adjustment. We're taking it slow."

"Hey, at least you're giving it a chance. Both of you. I believe it's going to work out just fine. And you know I'm not the happy ever after type." Bailey reminded him.

"I don't know about that," he'd told her. "That wedding at Basset Banks Wineries sure looked like a happy ever after for both you and Brynne."

Dane recalled that lovely double wedding as one of the first official Donovan family gatherings that he'd attended as an invited member of the family.

Bailey actually sighed at those words. "That was a beautiful day."

It had been and at the time Dane had wondered how many more beautiful days he would have with his newfound family.

"But that's not what you called about," Bailey said, sobering. "What do you need? And why does it need to be kept under wraps? Are you in some type of trouble?"

Dane had listened to the flurry of questions in awe because he'd never had anyone ask him anything with that hint of concern in their voice.

"I need you to do an in-depth background check on someone. I've done a preliminary google search but I didn't come up with much."

"And you think there's more to come up with?" she'd asked.

Dane's brows had drawn at her question. "Yeah, I do." He admitted.

"Okay, let me just grab a pen so I can take some notes."

A few seconds later, Bailey told him to proceed.

Dane had given her Zera's name and everything he knew about her, which sounded like absolutely nothing once he'd said it out loud. He would chastise himself later over getting involved with her twice without knowing a damn thing about her. At that moment, he just wanted Bailey to help him figure out what was going on.

"Are you sleeping with her?" Bailey had asked after the rundown of information.

He'd clenched his teeth before replying, "Yes. For the second time. I first met her here in Paris, four years ago."

Bailey whistled and Dane had let his head fall back as he'd inwardly groaned.

"Reunited lovers," she'd said. "In Paris. How totally romantic. If you're into that kind of stuff."

Bailey acted as if she weren't a romantic, but the mere fact that she'd mentioned it told Dane that she was. And her words had him once again asking what the hell he was doing.

"Just get me a detailed report, please. And remember to keep this between us."

He had no idea if he should be asking her to keep a secret when they'd only been related for a short time. But he had no other place to turn. If he hired another PI firm, there would be an official record of the arrangement. And while it was a PI firm's business to keep things private, Dane knew all too well how easily such information could serve in a blackmail or revenge plot. He wasn't willing to put himself in the middle of that type of scenario, again.

"No worries," she'd said. "I'm on the job and this will remain between us. Unless you're in danger, Dane. Then, all bets are off and I'll do whatever is necessary to keep you safe."

His chest had tightened at her words and his fingers had clenched the phone in an effort to keep his escalating emotions in check.

"I'm not in any danger, Bailey. But thanks. I appreciate your concern."

"You're family. We protect our own. Don't forget that, Dane. We're here, all of us. All you have to do is call."

He'd nodded and disconnected the call with his cousin before he said something he wouldn't be able to take back. Something that would solidify the fact that he was beginning to care a great deal about some of the members in his new family.

That conversation had taken place seven days ago. Zera had been staying at the hotel with Dane for six nights. She was there when he woke each morning and by the time he returned late afternoon or early evening, she was still there. Dane had no idea what she did during the time he was away. All he knew—and had been totally enamored with—was how attentive and mesmerizing she was. Even with that in mind, Dane couldn't help but think about how different things felt now with Zera.

Four years ago she'd been like a breath of fresh air. There'd been an exuberance and energy whenever he was around her. A feeling that, together, they were unstoppable. That sounded weird, especially to a man like Dane. He was a loner, an independent success in a world which had dealt him nothing but bad turns. Then, Zera had come along and for those two months she'd opened something inside of him, something that at the time had frightened and intrigued him. Now, after all that Dane had been through, Zera was no longer a refreshing change.

She was a burning need. Accompanied by a nagging sensation that was making Dane irritable.

Dane slammed on the brakes to keep from crashing into the car in front of him, which had also stopped suddenly. Cursing he let his head lull back against the seat and closed his eyes. He had to get a grip. Zera was not only meeting every sexual need Dane could have possibly imagined in the time she'd been staying at the hotel with him, but she was also draining him of every ounce of concentration. As evidenced by the meeting he'd just left with Roark and Suri.

"The resumes," Roark had said to Dane, the look on his face full of irritation.

"Two days ago you said you were going to review that last batch of resumes because you weren't satisfied with any of the candidates we'd interviewed so far for the executive liaison position. And now you're sitting here staring at that computer screen as if the candidate will magically morph from the screen to stand beside us and clinch the interview."

Dane had glanced across the nine-foot cherry wood dining table where they were set up in the suite, and stared at a clearly agitated Roark. The man's thick eyebrows were drawn, the pen he'd been holding in his hand now rolling across the table where he'd tossed it during his comments. Dane wasn't big on emotional outbursts, for any reason. He also did not like anyone raising their voice in business meetings. To him, it was never necessary. One could get their point across without needing to dominate the other through loud-speaking or dramatic gesturing.

But, Roark was right. Dane was distracted.

"I have narrowed it down to two candidates," Dane had replied. He reached into a folder he'd set on the table beside his laptop when the meeting first began.

He'd pulled out the copies of the resumes he'd made last night in the hotel's business center and passed them to Suri and Roark. Ridge was going to the airport to pick up their Aunt Birdie. A woman whom Dane was in no particular hurry to meet.

Dane was sure only a few moments had passed when Suri had punched him in the right shoulder. It was a surprisingly hard punch for a woman who looked as if she weighed no more than one hundred pounds soaking wet.

She'd chuckled and said, "I think it's a woman."

Dane had frowned and resisted the urge to rub his shoulder. "Both candidates are women."

Suri shook her head. Today's hairstyle was thick waves, parted on the side with one huge curl dangling over her forehead. It reminded him of one of the old black and white Josephine Baker pictures that hung in the study of his San Francisco house.

"Nope. It's another woman who has captured your thoughts to the point that you cannot focus on business."

When Dane didn't respond, Suri happily continued. "It's not a problem, you know. Everybody meets a person that takes them to the precipice of who they were and shows them who they can ultimately be. The real question is when do we get to meet her?"

There was no "her" for them, or anyone else to meet. It had taken Dane half an hour to convince Suri of that and to get on with the rest of the meeting. Roark hadn't said anything about his sister's summation, but Dane noticed the continued questioning in the man's gaze as he looked at him. Dane decided he didn't care what they thought of him, or what assumptions Suri had made. They were wrapping up their business anyway. With members of the Board of Directors in place—industry professionals that both Roark and Dane had recommended—and a detailed plan for how Donovan Oilwell International would directly correlate with Donovan Oilwell UK, the Donovan Oilwell branches in the States and Imagine Energy Corporation, the start-up process was just about complete. The executive liaison would be responsible for making sure the continued correlation between all the entities went smoothly.

Dane and Roark would be named CEOs of Donovan Oilwell International, but Roark would oversee the daily operation. Ridge would step into Roark's previous role as CEO of Donovan Oilwell UK and Suri would take on her first official position since passing her final aptitude tests. She would serve as the official chartered accountant to the new company.

At that point, Dane's business in Paris would be complete. As for the relaxation portion of his trip, Dane could thank Zera for taking care of that.

Dane was still thinking about Zera when he'd finally made it back to his hotel. He parked the car and sat for another moment staring through the windshield. Zera had turned into a big part of this trip. It was not intentional and yet, that was the truth of the matter. Which was why hearing from Bailey was so imperative.

Zera was not the same as she had been before. There was a hint of worry and, to Dane's dismay, fear, in her eyes. He wanted to know why, even though he had no idea what he planned to do with the information. He only knew that finding out what was going on with her was now a priority. One which he would reconcile with himself later. For now, he could not wait to get back to his room and see her again.

"Where are you?" Aasir asked the moment Zera answered the burner phone that had been delivered to Ines two days ago.

Dane had meetings every day which made it much easier for Zera to do the things she needed to do without him being around and possibly asking too many questions. She'd met Ines yesterday at Onze Homme, an Afropolitan boutique and café located in Little Africa, part of the 18th Arrondissement, to pick up the rest of her clothes from her apartment and the package that Aasir had sent.

"I am safe," she told him.

Each evening Dane returned to the hotel at different times, so earlier today, Zera had put in an order for their food and asked the man at the front desk to call the room when Dane was on his way up and have the food delivered fifteen minutes after. That call had come just a few seconds before Aasir's.

Zera planned to start their evening the same way she had on the previous evenings, by asking about his day. She was always careful not to pry too deeply into Dane's life as she did not want to risk him asking her more questions in return. He'd already asked one question that she successfully avoided. Guilt sat like a rock in her chest as Zera recalled Dane asking the real reason why she bribed someone to get into his room that first night after they'd slept together. She pretended to be asleep that night and thankfully, Dane had not pressed the issue in the morning, or any of the days following. But Zera knew he was wondering. He was too smart a man not to.

"Safe is relative," Aasir continued. I want to know where you are. I can send someone in to get you out," he insisted.

Zera had known Aasir since she was a young girl. His family lived in the suburban Nairobi area of Gigiri, just as Zera's had. But when Zera had left to attend college in the States, Aasir had stayed. They'd kept in touch via letters, Skype calls and the one time Aasir had visited Washington, D.C. They shared a very special friendship that Zera appreciated and cherished.

"I am still in Paris," she finally stated because she knew he was not going to let it go.

Zera also knew that Aasir would definitely send someone to come get her and return her to Nairobi, because despite what he'd said before, that was the only place Aasir considered Zera's home.

He sighed and she acknowledged his frustration.

"You must get out of there, Zera. It is not safe for you. Not now that we know they are looking for you," he insisted.

"But why?" she asked. "Why are they looking for me? I have been under the radar since Emmet's death. Making no contact with anyone from the last four years. I was out of the spotlight that Emmet had put me in. So why come for me now? What do they want?"

"You know as well as I do that they only have two goals, more money and more death. It comes down to those two things."

Zera did not tell Aasir about the money she had taken from Emmet's safe before leaving the condo that they'd shared. She also did not tell him about the agenda book she'd found in the safe as well. The one with the names and phone numbers of all of Emmet's contacts.

"You cannot commit the rest of your life to this. It is over now. You must come home."

"It is not over until Hiari is safe."

"She may already be dead," Aasir said with finality.

Zera did not respond.

"You must accept that the possibility of that truth is there. It has been five years since she was taken. Why would they keep her alive?"

"Money," Zera replied. "You just said that is one of their goals. More and more money."

As she said those words Zera hoped with all that was within her that she was right. Hiari was only fourteen when she had been taken. Whenever Zera closed her eyes she could still see her pretty face, filled with a fresh innocence that Zera prayed had not been taken away also. She prayed that even if—no, that once she found Hiari, that her younger cousin would be able to forget these past five years and move on to live the promising life that her parents and the rest of Zera's family had envisioned for her.

"It is time for you to stop. You cannot do this alone."

"No one else will do it!" Zera yelled.

She looked through the open bedroom door. Dane was on his way upstairs and she did not want to be on the phone when he arrived.

"No one is looking for her. Not the President or the Minister of State Security and certainly not the United States government," she told Aasir.

"You know that there is much bureaucracy in these matters," Aasir countered. "Is that not what you studied in that big fancy American school?"

Zera rubbed the center of her forehead where a headache

was brewing. She paced back and forth across the bedroom floor.

"None of the funding that has reportedly been sent to assist with the widespread kidnappings in Africa is helping to find Hiari. They claim to be focused on shutting down the groups they have now glorified by identifying them as a Foreign Terrorist Organization, but how many of the victims are actually returned to their families? What has happened to all those girls taken throughout our country? Nobody has an answer. My family needs an answer," she said adamantly, tears stinging her eyes and clogging her throat.

Aasir sighed heavily. "I know what you are saying. I am still trying to help. But I cannot protect you from here. I need you to return to safety."

Zera heard a noise in the outer room. Dane was home. She waited only a few seconds before walking across the bedroom and into the bathroom, where she closed the door behind her.

"I am safe. I am staying with a friend that nobody knows of. So I will be fine as soon as I finish searching for the name listed on the registration plate of the car that tried to run me down," Zera whispered.

"A friend? Is this friend a male or female?" Aasir asked.

"He is an American. That is all I can say right now. Keep this phone. I will call you again soon."

Zera did not wait for Aasir's response. She tucked the phone into the back pocket of her shorts and turned on the water in the sink. She washed her hands after leaning forward to splash water onto her face. Grabbing a towel she dried her face and hands and looked into the mirror.

Who was she? Not the idealistic young woman who had graduated from college with her law degree and eagerly stepped into a career in America. No, that smiling and ambitious person was gone. Leaving this one who lived with secrets and walked in danger. The one with a sole purpose in her life and no time to entertain anything or anyone else.

Even the sexy and debonair Dane Donovan who was probably now at this very moment waiting on the other side of that door, wondering who the person on the other side was as well?

Zera had no answers for him. And she had no time to think of ones that she might want to give him.

CHAPTER 8

"*On Izhets. Ubey yego!*"

Misha threw back his head and emptied the glass of vodka. He slammed the glass down onto the table with a clunk, and ignored Luka even though there was merit in his brigadier's words. The man sitting across from them wearing the expensive suit and diamonds at his ears and on his fingers, was a liar. And he should be killed for continuing to lie to Misha's face. Men had done less and been dismembered on Misha's orders. But this situation was unique. The stakes were higher this time. The one Misha really wanted was still free to breathe. For now, that was the priority.

"I do not reward mistakes," Misha said, his voice calm considering the circumstances.

"We've got this under control," the man replied.

His name was Urod, or freak in Misha's native Russian language. He had another name, but it was something that Misha could not pronounce and thus Misha had taken to calling the man Urod. The man answered to the name because he knew what was best for him. He also knew who put thousands of dollars in cash in his hands on a weekly basis.

Misha stared down at his hands. There was a hangnail. He frowned. That bitch had not done a good job on his manicure. She would pay for that. Misha was very careful about his appearance. He wore only the most expensive suits, silk ties, gold and diamonds on his fingers, Italian leather shoes on his feet. His brown hair was tapered on the sides and much longer on top, but always neat. The lady he paid for a daily shave was good at her job and always kept his beard groomed. The two women who occupied his bed each night were also good at their job. Thinking about them made Misha anxious to finish his business and return to the hotel.

"I want her found," Misha said before giving the waitress a curt nod.

She had nice tits, but no ass which is why she was only serving drinks instead of being up on stage like the other lovelies Misha had personally selected. The club brought in close to $250,000 weekly. This amount included revenue from cover charges, drinks and the private subscriptions which were Luka's idea. Men with very deep pockets and ridiculous titles in whichever country they originated from, paid good money to be part of this club. And Misha was proud to provide excellent entertainment for them. The drugs that were distributed through the back rooms was an added bonus. And that revenue was counted separately in Misha's organization.

Misha drank from the new glass the waitress brought to him. He let the bitter liquor settle in the back of his throat while staring at her tits again. She knew not to move until he gave her permission. He licked his lips as the dark circle of her nipple was visible through the tight white t-shirt she was instructed to wear.

He wanted to touch her nipple with his tongue. He could suck tits all day and night. His dick hardened and he shifted uncomfortably in his seat.

"You bring her to me. I want her standing in front of me just like this," Misha said to Urod.

Misha reached out to cup her breast in the palm of his hand. She made a sound and he yelled, "*Tsi-shih-NAH!*"

She looked away but Misha did not care. All his girls were trained to be quiet. There was never a need for them to speak. Just stand and wait to provide pleasure. He did not even know the language this one spoke. It was not Russian or English and Misha did not care. She belonged to him and that was all that mattered.

"I've got a man at her house," Urod told him.

"But she is not there," Misha continued, his voice returning to its calm gravely tone. "I too have men at her house. She has not been there in days."

Urod leaned back in his chair. His eyes grazed over the backside of the waitress. With his free hand Misha pushed the table so that it rammed into Urod's chest, pinning the skinny man against the back wall. While Urod wheezed his next breath, Misha tweaked the waitress's nipple. Misha's mouth watered.

"One day," Misha said and ripped the shirt from the waitress. "I want her in front of me in one day."

Urod was still gasping for breath when Misha pulled the waitress closer. Luka would escort him out of the club now that Misha was finished talking to him. Misha yanked on the waitress's arm until she bent over in front of him. He stuck out his tongue, his body going tight with intense pleasure the second his tongue touched her nipple. He lifted the now bare breast in his hand, enjoying the contrast between their skin tones immensely. Hers was darker, so very dark. While his was white, pure. His chubby fingers moved roughly over her skin as he now juggled both her breasts in his hands. He loved to see them shake. They were so heavy and sat up so high on her.

Behind him he heard the music start. His already growing erection was now stiff as a stick against his thigh. He pulled the waitress down onto his lap and turned in his seat so that he could see the stage.

Right on schedule, the house lights dimmed, and white spotlights appeared on the stage. His hands gripped the waitress's breasts while her head fell back against his shoulder. She sobbed. Misha did not care. On the stage three new girls appeared. They were young and precious. Not really Misha's thing since their bodies had not been developed to the lushness he favored. But the crowd loved them. There would be much money made tonight as the guests bid for who they would spend a couple of hours with. This was a good batch, he thought as he maneuvered the waitress to sit over his erection.

These girls had come in last week's shipment from China. He had yet to find another contact in Africa, after Luka had taken care of the one that was Emmet's supplier. The deal with Emmet had been lucrative, for a while. Then the man became greedy and sloppy, two things Misha did not tolerate.

The waitress was stiff. She did not move the way he needed. She was not trying. With a growl Misha pushed her off of him and she tumbled to the floor. He stood up and motioned toward the door. His driver would follow him out now and Misha would instruct him to take him back to the hotel. He would return to the house where he lived part-time on the French Riviera once Emmet's friend—the woman named Zera—was in his custody.

For now, he would leave this place, the club he'd named The

Grande. And he would not return for a while. They needed new staff. He would have Luka tend to that before he could come back.

Minutes later Misha slipped into the back seat of the white car. He unzipped his pants and freed his stiff length. Letting his head fall back onto the leather seats he worked his hand over his cock, searching for enough relief to whet his appetite for tonight. The lovelies that were waiting for him were voracious. He needed longevity to be on his side, without the help of any drug.

When he closed his eyes, moaning with the spikes of pleasure already streaking through his body, Misha saw her face. The tall black woman who had stood beside Emmet on the last night that Misha had seen the man alive. She'd worn a very short skirt and he could picture her long legs wrapped around his waist. He would love to watch them through the mirror above his bed at his home. Their coloring would be intoxicating, her body more than enjoyable, more than…his release came quick, spurting onto his hands and pants as his leg shook and his moans filled the interior of the car.

Urod had one day to get Misha what he wanted and then there would be more death. Until Misha had everything due to him and nothing less.

There were candles. Fragrant ones, Dane noted as he walked deeper into the hotel room. The curtains at the windows were drawn. The table—which still held enjoyable memories for him—was now covered with a white linen cloth. Short, fat candles in a circle of three were lit in the center of the table. White plates with matching napkins, wine glasses and shined silverware accompanied the candles.

Dane set his briefcase on the couch and removed his suit jacket. He loosened his tie and listened carefully to the low murmur of her voice. She was in the bedroom, on the phone he surmised. He walked closer. She spoke in hushed tones and Dane wondered who she was talking to.

"My family needs an answer," she'd said.

Dane continued forward and was almost to the doorway of the bedroom when he heard a door close. He stopped then, realizing that she had gone into the bathroom. So that he would not hear her conversation? He frowned and resisted the urge to storm into the room and insist she open the door. He could demand answers from her. Push the issue until she told him everything. Because Dane was certain she had something to tell.

Was she on the run from an abusive husband?

No, he'd told himself this earlier. She'd been involved romantically with Emmet up until six months ago when he'd died. Dane had googled his former friend and came up with nothing about his death. There hadn't been much online about Emmet Parks when he was living either. But that wasn't foremost on Dane's mind.

Zera was a hacker and she apparently had no problem bribing people to do her bidding. Did that make her a cop, or maybe she was an informant? She was definitely using his room to hide from someone. Dane had figured that the evening after she'd arrived and a delivery man had brought a duffle bag with her belongings inside. She'd told him the older woman she'd been staying with had sent her things and that she was going to be looking for a new apartment. Dane hadn't believed her, but he hadn't asked the pertinent questions either.

He wondered why?

What was it about this woman that had him deciding that it was better to have her lying next to him in bed each night, than wondering where she was sleeping and who she might be sleeping with? What was it that had him tossing out all the parameters he'd so studiously operated within while involved in sexual relationships with other women?

More questions.

Dane rubbed a hand down the back of his head and stepped into the bedroom. He set on the edge of the bed, his back to the bathroom door and pulled the tie from around his neck. He began to unbutton his shirt and was just pulling it off when the bathroom door opened.

"Hey," she said in a breezy, casual tone.

"Hey," Dane replied, his voice somber compared to hers.

"I ordered dinner for us," she continued.

He could hear her moving on the other side of the room. She unzipped her bag and zipped it again.

"Good," he answered. "I'm hungry."

"Me too. I had some errands to run today so I did not get a chance to get lunch," she told him. "It should arrive in a few minutes. I told room service to deliver at six forty-five."

Dane nodded. He removed his shoes and stood up to undo his belt and then take off his pants. When he was about to walk the pants to the closet to place them on a hanger, he saw her leaning against the doorjamb. She wore denim shorts that probably could have used a few more inches of material to stretch down her thighs. Her feet were bare, her top, a pink sleeveless design that hugged her breasts and stopped abruptly to leave her midriff bare. She'd created some type of braid with her hair and pulled it so that it rested over one shoulder. With no make-up on her face and her arms crossed over her chest, she looked young, pretty and carefree.

Dane walked to the closet without saying another word.

"Did your business go okay today?" she asked.

He'd just draped the pants over a hanger and put them into the closet.

"It's coming along," he told her. And then, for reasons he did not want to explore, Dane continued. "This new venture is a big undertaking. I've been involved with new start-ups before, but this one seems different."

"Because it is with your family?"

His head whipped around at her question as he wondered just how much Zera knew about him. Dane would be the first to admit that he was not a talkative man. He did not share his life easily. Probably because his life had been so unusual for so long.

"Yes," he admitted. "I'm not entirely sure how to deal with these new relatives on a business, or a personal level."

It was the first time he'd said that aloud.

Dane went to the dresser. He removed his watch and set it next to his bottle of cologne and deodorant. His leather toiletry bag was opened but empty. The shaving supplies he carried in it were in the bathroom. Beside the bag was Zera's deodorant, bottles filled with colorful perfumes, lotions, a travel size manicure set and earrings. She had a few pair of earrings in different sizes. The ones she wore right now were gold studs in a 3D square shape.

"Just be yourself," she said. "That's what my grandmother used to tell me. Whenever I had to meet new people she would say just be yourself. They either like you or they don't, either way it is their problem, not yours."

After he'd opened one of the drawers, pulled out a pair of basketball shorts and put them on, Dane looked at her again.

The fact that he was so intrigued by her, that he wanted nothing more but to pick her up and toss her fine ass onto that bed and sink his length into her once more, was totally his problem. There was no denying that.

"Do you have trouble being yourself around new people, Zera?" Dane asked as he closed the distance between them.

She pushed away from the doorjamb until she was standing straight in front of him. "There are many different parts of being me," she said before leaning in to drop a quick kiss on the tip of his nose.

When Dane would have said something else, there was a knock at the door.

"Dinner's here," she said before turning and heading out to the living area.

Dane followed her and watched as she helped the delivery guy move the covered dishes from his cart to set on the neatly decorated table. It struck him then how domestic this scene appeared. They could have easily been mistaken for a couple on vacation. Maybe that's what the delivery guy thought when Zera reached into her back pocket and pulled out folded euros. She handed them to him and he smiled, muttering, "*Merci,*" before he stepped out of the room.

Zera replied, her French just as smooth and fluent as the man's had been.

"*Mon plaisir. Bonne soirée,*" she'd said as she closed and locked the door.

Dane moved closer to the table. He pulled out a chair and motioned for her to have a seat. When she did, he let his hands rest on her shoulders and looked down to the top of her head.

"*Tu n'es pas né à Paris. Quand as-tu appris à parler français?*" he asked, wanting to know when she had learned to speak French.

She waited a beat before replying, "*Je suis né à Nairobi. Je parle couramment le français, l'allemand et le russe.*"

So she spoke French, German and Russian. Did she just have an interest in foreign languages?

Dane let his hands fall away from her shoulders. He circled the table and took the seat across from her. She was already removing the covers from each dish.

"I figured we'd have some American favorites tonight," she announced. "Cheeseburgers and French fries, which is a false statement since the first claim to potatoes being fried came from Belgium."

"History and foreign languages," Dane said as he placed his napkin in his lap. "You're quite eclectic."

She'd just set a cheeseburger with chunky pickles and thick melted cheese onto her plate. She used her napkin to wipe her hands before looking up at him. For endless seconds she did not speak and Dane took the other burger from the dish and placed it on the plate in front of him. He also took some of the fries, placing them beside his burger. Then he looked at her again.

"I guess you could say that," she replied with a shrug. "You also speak French."

Dane nodded. He usually preferred his burger with fried onions and barbeque sauce, but he was fine with what she'd ordered for him.

"I was inspired after my first trip to Paris four years ago," he replied and had the pleasure of watching her mouth open and then shut quickly because she obviously did not know how to respond.

For the next few moments they ate in silence, until the new

questions that continued to pop into Dane's mind, would not be contained.

"Tell me about your family. Are you an only child? What are your parents like? Do they mind that you live here in Paris and not at home with them?"

Zera had finished her fries but still had about half her burger to go. Dane enjoyed being with a woman who ate. The constant diet fads and body-shaming that went with women of different sizes was exhausting and wrong on so many levels. While Zera had a model-slim body, it wasn't from lack of eating. After spending this past week with her, Dane could attest to that fact.

"I'm an only child," she replied. "Just like you."

He shook his head. "I have two sisters now," Dane said. "My other sister was killed a year ago."

"And by "now" you mean because you found out who your biological father is."

Dane was only marginally shocked that she knew about that. The Donovans were known worldwide and the story of Bailey's kidnapping and its connection to the paternity test had made national news.

"Yes," he told her. "My paternal father and I were joined by a paternity test. With those results also came more siblings. Aunts, uncles, and cousins as well."

"You do not sound as if you consider that a good thing."

"It is," Dane said. "That is how this new business venture came to be. So I am grateful for that."

"Is everything about business with you, Dane? What about your personal life? What about you just taking time to be you?"

She'd done it again, and not as smoothly as she probably thought she had. Zera always steered his questions away from her. She would give him just a little of herself and then pull back. But that was only in one area, Dane thought as he finished his burger and sat back in his chair. There was one particular way in which Zera could not hold back or hide her feelings from him.

"Are you finished?" Dane asked.

He was standing before she could answer.

"Yes," she replied. "I guess so."

Dane reached for her hand. When she placed it in his, he pulled her up from the chair. He didn't have to tell her what he wanted. Zera knew because she wanted it too. In this area, they had that type of communication where the words weren't really necessary. So this was the area Dane told himself to focus on. It was the place where he had some control.

Zera placed a hand on his cheek and Dane leaned into the warmth of her touch. He turned his face so that he could kiss her palm, before wrapping his arms around her waist and pulling her closer. She grabbed his shoulders and he kissed her, his tongue immediately dueling with hers. This kiss wasn't normal. Dane knew this instantly. Nothing between them was normal. The hunger they had for each other never seemed to be sated. Instead, he fed off her desire for him like she was a feast and he was always famished.

As if on cue she lowered her arms and pushed at his shorts. Dane moved her hands away.

"Not yet," he told her after tearing his mouth away from hers.

He ignored her questioning gaze and pulled that piece of a shirt up and over her head in seconds. Her unbound breasts bounced and he groaned. It took tremendous restraint, but Dane did not touch them. Instead he pulled the snap of her shorts open and pushed them down her legs. She flattened her hands on his back as he leaned over and allowed her to take each leg out of the shorts. On his way up, Dane placed an open-mouthed kiss over the swatch of pale pink silk that covered her mound.

When he stood, he took her mouth again, sucking her tongue deep into his mouth. She clasped her arms around the back of his neck, her hands flattening on his head. She pressed into him and every part of Dane's body hardened. *Not yet*, he had to tell himself. The words played over and over in his mind as he continued to drown in her kisses. She was so sexual, so amazingly in tune with everything he liked. At least Dane hoped that would continue to be the case.

He broke the kiss finally, giving himself only a few seconds to catch his breath before grabbing her hand and telling her to, "Come."

Dane walked her back through the bedroom and into the bathroom. He switched on the water in the shower before removing his shirt. Zera stepped to him, dipping her head so that her lips and tongue could meet his tight nipple. Dane let her continue as he pushed at his shorts. She picked up there, moving the shorts and his boxer briefs down to his ankles and waiting while he stepped out of them. She reached for him and Dane looked down to see her slim fingers wrapped around his veiny dick. He wanted to push her to her knees and let her bring him the pleasure he craved, but again, he refrained.

Moving out of her grasp, Dane stepped into the shower and waited for her to do the same. She removed her thong and joined him.

He grabbed a sponge and poured liquid soap over it. He washed her, starting at her neck and going down over her breasts, under her arms, down her torso and then between her legs.

"Shhh, baby. I know what you need," he told her when she gasped at his touch.

Dane continued to run the soapy sponge over her body. And when he was finished he switched places so that she was under the spray of hot water. She tilted her head back to keep her hair from getting wet. He stood behind her, using his hands in conjunction with the water to clean her body of the soap. She leaned back against him and once again the punch of reality hit him with force.

They were acting like a normal couple enjoying their private time in Paris. Is this what it felt like to be involved in a committed relationship? Coming in from work to dinner with her and now showering with her? What was next?

Dane had that answer.

After allowing her to return the favor of washing him, Dane and Zera stepped out of the shower. He dried her body and then wrapped the thick plush towel around her. He dried himself and walked them out to the bedroom.

"Is this dessert?" Zera asked when they were standing at the foot of the bed.

He looked at her, tendrils of hair that had gotten wet anyway stuck to her forehead and temple. Her lips were swollen from his kisses. Dane pulled the towel away from her.

"You're *my* dessert, Zera," he said before picking her up and dropping her onto the bed.

CHAPTER 9

*D*ane Donovan was a man of his word.

Zera's fingers clenched the duvet beneath her while the heels of her feet dug into the mattress. Dane was kneeling at the bottom of the bed, his strong hands clamped onto her ass cheeks as he held her to his mouth and feasted on her as if she were, in fact, the top dessert offered on the menu tonight.

"Oh. Oh. Oh!" she whispered, then wailed as his tongue moved over sensitive flesh and created a slurping rhythm that she knew she'd never forget.

It was as if he were purposely being loud and fast, pushing her already burning arousal to higher heights. Zera was panting now, her thighs quivering as he continued to lick and suck. A magical finger pressed against her clit and circled in quick motions that had her hips lifting from the bed, as she grinded wantonly into his face.

Heat soared through her body, landing with accurate precision between her legs and at her aching nipples. Zera pulled her hands away from the duvet to cup her breasts. They felt heavy and full and she moaned as her own touch brought on even more pleasure. With her thumb and finger she squeezed each nipple and moved her hands so that they shook. Her breath was coming in heavy pants now, her arms and legs shaking as she grew closer to her release.

This was unlike anything Zera had ever felt before. Sure, she'd pleasured herself more times than she could count and even then, knowing her body as only she could, there was nothing as fiery and intense as she was feeling right at this moment.

His fingers were moving alongside his tongue, one still working her clit, the other gliding through the thick essence flowing from her, coating her plump folds. He'd pushed her back a little, so that her feet were now a couple inches off the bed, her legs spread even wider as he stayed positioned between them. When he pushed two fingers into her, scissoring them so that she felt him against her honey coated walls with on-and-off pressure, Zera groaned loud and long. Her toes clenched, fingers squeezing her nipples until tears stung her eyes. How could even the pain feel so good?

Zera was in no way prepared for how that question would continue to resonate in her mind.

Not until Dane's fingers moved, spreading her now constantly flowing juices down to that forbidden place he'd touched so many times throughout this week. Almost every time they were together, he touched her there. That first night it had been just a brush of his fingers and she was so caught up in the ecstasy of the moment, Zera had actually thought it was a mistake. But then the next night as he'd pressed her back against the wall of the shower and she'd wrapped one leg around his waist. He'd slammed his dick into her while his hand came down from her ass to press a finger inside that illicit spot. There'd been more touches, more probing that again, she'd dismissed because everything else had felt so damn good.

Tonight, Zera thought differently.

He was continually touching her there, as if he were purposely moistening the area for something…more. Her pulse quickened with the thought, her tongue snaking out to swipe over her now dry lips. She released her nipples, her hands slamming down onto the mattress as his tongue thrust inside her entrance, two of his fingers applying pressure to the other place.

"You want it, don't you?"

His voice was thick as he spoke between licking.

Zera's body shook. What was he asking her?

She couldn't think straight. Couldn't figure out what was happening. All she knew was that whatever it was, it felt good. Too good.

"Yeah, you do," he said, pulling back slightly and blowing over her clit. "You know what's coming and you can't wait."

Zera shook her head. It was an impulse. She heard his words and a part of her said "no" he was wrong. She didn't want it. Wait, what was it that she didn't want?"

He moved away from her and she actually cried out. The loss of him near her and the incompletion that instantly filled her brought forth an immediate reaction.

"What are you doing?" she asked, coming up on her elbows, mind still foggy with desire.

"Shhhh," was his reply.

He was moving to the chair closest to the dresser where she'd noticed a bag that he must have brought in with him while she'd been in the bathroom earlier. He was beautifully naked and for a few quiet seconds she took in the magnificence of his body from the back. His shoulders were wide and swollen with muscle that stretched down his back to a tight ass with matching indentations on each side. His thighs and biceps screamed strength, and when he turned to face her, his long, thick erection bobbed and extended as if calling to her personally.

Zera swallowed hard. Her mouth watered and she swallowed again.

"Yeah," he said. He nodded his head as he walked toward the bed. "You definitely want it."

Yes, she wanted that dick. There was absolutely no question about that. But something told Zera, Dane was talking about something else. Something darker and illicit, wicked and for whatever reason, she thought, sexy as hell.

"Get on your knees," he said when he was once again standing at the foot of the bed.

Zera hesitated. She was no stranger to him hitting it doggy-style. She'd learned this week that, it, along with her riding him, were Dane's preferred positions. Zera was cool with that. Even though she loved being able to wrap her legs around his waist, holding him close to her when they both tumbled into their climax together. There was a certain primal enjoyment from him standing behind and pumping into her with all his strength.

"What is that?" she asked when her gaze fell to the black box and tube he'd set on the bed.

"It's for you," he replied. "I couldn't stop thinking about you this morning, so I made a stop before going to my meeting."

"A present? For me?"

Zera knew she sounded foolish. The box wasn't gift-wrapped and the tube, looked like tooth paste or some sort of ointment, or...her pulse tripped again and her clit throbbed.

"It's all for you," Dane said.

He stood there as if he were actually offering her everything. His body and whatever was in that box. She could have it, all she had to do was take it. Zera didn't know what to do. That wasn't accurate. She knew. She only prayed it wasn't the wrong decision.

But how could it be wrong? If she felt so damn good just thinking about it. Anticipating and needing…

She sat up, keeping her gaze locked on Dane's as she slowly turned away from him, pushing herself up onto her knees. Her arms shook slightly as she flattened her palms on the mattress to evenly distribute her weight. Her ass was in the air, her legs spread slightly so that he now had a clear view of her ass and her pussy. A shiver ran through her, a cool slice so thrilling and wickedly pleasurable, she bit her lower lip to keep from screaming out before he ever touched her.

"Do you trust me, Zera?"

She heard the question as his palm rested heavily on her right butt cheek.

Zera inhaled deeply and released the breath slowly. "Yes," she said, acknowledging to herself that she actually did trust Dane. Moreso, than she had ever thought she would trust someone who wasn't her family.

"I'll only do what's pleasurable," he continued.

She nodded as his other palm rested on her left cheek. Then he was pulling them apart. It was a slow, but definitely delicious sensation that ran through her with the knowledge that he was looking at a very private part of her. What was he thinking? Feeling? Her breasts dangled, nipples still taut.

He was still for endless seconds and just when she was about to turn her head to see what he was doing, Zera felt one of his hands move and then the other. He was moving behind her and the next thing she felt was coolness that had her gasping. The lube touched the skin of her sphincter as he pushed one cheek to the side and rubbed his finger over her.

Zera's arms shook and she licked her lips. It felt good. Cool. Sensual. Forbidden.

"Whatever is pleasurable," he whispered, his finger slipping past the tight rim to move slowly inside of her.

She audibly sucked in a breath at that point. Dane removed his finger quickly. Zera tried to steady her breathing. She knew what he was doing. There was no mistaking now. The question was, how much more would she take? Could she do this? Had she ever considered doing this before?

He was opening the box and she did turn to look at him at that point. The top was off the box and inside were three silver items, stark and shining against the dark interior. He picked up one, the smallest, and coated it with lube. A part of her wanted to bolt. She should have rolled off the bed and run for cover. Another part, the darker side that she had no idea existed until this moment, kept her gaze focused on that silver item.

"Tell me to stop," he said.

He was looking directly at her now.

"If you don't want this, tell me to stop right now."

Zera blinked. She licked her lips again and told herself how strong and confident she was. How she wanted Dane and whatever pleasure he could bring her. How whatever small bits of fear might be dancing around inside of her were normal, but not necessary. She did not speak, but turned her head so that she was once again looking ahead, but not at Dane.

Her silence was her acquiescence.

He caressed her ass, slapping one cheek until a slight stinging had her clenching her teeth. Then she felt his finger again, circling around her, pressing slowly inside and pulling out. In again, this time with two fingers. When she jumped, he whispered, "Relax, baby. I got you."

Zera breathed in and out as if she were a star pupil in one of those Lamaze classes. Next was more coolness as something hard pressed against her rim. Her fingers clenched in the duvet, her eyes closed tightly.

"It's going to feel so good," Dane was saying. "Just you wait, you're never going to forget this feeling. Or who gave it to you."

Right now she was having a hard time wrapping her mind around the stretching of this tight space. The feeling that she was being opened and simultaneously filled made her dizzy. She was nodding her head even though he hadn't asked her a question. She couldn't speak, could only feel...and there was so much to feel. So much that she'd never imagined.

"So good, baby. You're taking it all because you're so good. And you were ready for this," he said and pushed it in further.

Was she ready? Zera had no idea, but with one last nudge the silver plug he'd taken from that box was snugly inside of her. Dane rubbed her ass. He kissed one cheek and then the next.

"It's so pretty, baby."

There were red hearts on the end of each plug. Zera recalled glimpsing that much. But she could not imagine how it looked inserted inside of her. All she knew was how it felt. And she was amazed that now there was no pain. Just a delicious eroticism that snaked through her like long silky fingers. She felt like purring with the sensation, but instead, dipped her back lower, rolling her head on her shoulders as if preparing for the next step.

And that step came quickly as Dane sheathed his dick,

grabbed her hips and thrust deep and fast into her. Zera gasped. If she'd thought she felt full before, now she was certain she would explode with pleasure at any moment.

"Hold on," he directed and once again, Zera followed his instructions.

He hadn't led her wrong up to this point. And once he began moving, fucking her with every ounce of strength he had in his glorious body, that statement was affirmed.

"Dane!"

His name had become a chant as Zera grabbed the duvet and sheet pulling them both off the mattress. He was still pumping when her legs wobbled and gave out, her orgasm pouring from her in a gush and tremors throughout her body. He'd climbed on the bed, still holding her hips, lifting her ass up off the bed as he continued to pound into her. He was saying something. She loved hearing his voice, hearing how into this he was, but for the life of her Zera couldn't understand what he was saying. Hell, she wasn't even sure she could say her name or recite the alphabet at this moment. And when he finally held her ass close to him, pressing all of his length deep inside of her so that his orgasm could pulsate through his body, Zera came again. This time she didn't call his name. She whispered something to herself instead, "Don't fall in love with him."

Dane spent his first free morning in the last week working out at the hotel gym. As with the previous nights that Zera had been there, last night he'd slept comfortably and soundly. She'd been curled in his arms. A position he'd come to learn that she liked because if at some point during the night they parted, she would search for him. Even going so far as to nudge him in the back when he was turned away from her, waiting until he turned over again and then easing into his arms once more. The first and last woman Dane had ever slept with had been Zera. It made sense that the only woman he enjoyed sleeping with be her as well.

But when he'd awakened this morning Zera had been gone. Not as in, never coming back. He'd been alarmed for about ten minutes until he'd seen that her duffel bag and the personal items she kept on the dresser were still there. Her gray backpack, the one she always kept with her, was of course, gone. But she had obviously gotten up and dressed without waking him. Dane sat on the side of the bed for another half hour wondering about where she was and why she'd felt it necessary to leave without telling him. At that point he'd decided that he was wasting time. Zera was going to do whatever it was she was doing. Dane sensed that there may be a reason she wasn't telling him exactly what that was.

So he'd pulled on a pair of shorts, a t-shirt, and his tennis shoes. He went downstairs to the gym. There, he'd spent the next two and a half hours. Forty minutes after that he'd done laps at the pool. And then he'd sat on one of the lounge chairs and pulled his cell phone out of the bag he'd brought down with him that also contained two bottles of water.

He frowned when he saw that Bailey had sent an email marked by that irritating red exclamation point. It was urgent. Dane's finger hovered over the screen of his phone for a few seconds before he finally decided to press the button to open the message.

Dane read the email, scrolling down when his screen was too small to see the entire message at one time. The muscles in his jaw clenched as he absorbed what his cousin was telling him.

ZERA SIDIKA KENNEDY WAS BORN FEBRUARY 28, 1988 TO NENJI JACINTA KENNEDY IN NAIROBI, KENYA. NO FATHER IS MENTIONED ON THE OFFICIAL DOCUMENTS. SHE IS OF MAASAI DESCENT AND WAS RAISED IN A MIDDLE-CLASS SUBURBAN AREA WHERE SHE ATTENDED SCHOOL. SHE CAME TO THE UNITED STATES FOR COLLEGE, GRADUATING FROM TUSKEGEE UNIVERSITY WHERE SHE MAJORED IN POLITICAL SCIENCE AND INTERNATIONAL AFFAIRS. SHE ALSO HAS A LAW DEGREE FROM STANFORD UNIVERSITY.

ALL INFORMATION STOPS HERE.

THERE IS NOTHING ON HER DMV RECORDS, NO CRIMINAL RECORD, NO FINANCIAL TRACES OF HER ANYWHERE. YOU SAY YOU MET HER IN PARIS FOUR YEARS AGO. THAT WOULD BE ABOUT A YEAR AND A HALF AFTER SHE GRADUATED FROM STANFORD. TO FALL OFF THE GRID THE WAY SHE DID WITH NO HISTORY OF CRIMINAL OR IMMIGRATION ISSUES, IN MY OPINION, POINTS TO DOMESTIC VIOLENCE.

IF YOU NEED TO KNOW MORE WE MAY NEED TO CALL IN TRENT. HE HAS MORE UNDERGROUND ACCESS THAN WE ARE ALLOWED TO USE LEGALLY THROUGH D&D. BOTH HE AND DEVLIN HAVE RESOURCES AROUND THE WORLD THAT THEY COULD EASILY HIT UP TO DIG DEEPER INTO HER LIFE.

LET ME KNOW HOW YOU WANT TO PROCEED.

BAILEY

Dane read the message three times. Each time digesting the small glimpse into the life of the woman he was sleeping with.

Hadn't he already been thinking that she was running from

someone? But what about Emmet? Had she run from one man, into the arms of another? And what had those two months between her and Dane been?

He typed a response to Bailey.

I APPRECIATE YOU GETTING THIS INFORMATION FOR ME. DON'T INVOLVE TRENT. I'LL FIGURE THE REST OUT ON MY OWN. THANKS FOR YOUR HELP.

He did not sign the message with his name, nor did he give any explanation of what he planned to do next. Dane stuffed his phone back into the bag and stood to leave. He walked away from the pool area, through a long hallway leading to the elevators and rode up to his room. All the while thinking that he'd had enough. Secrets, betrayal and everything that inevitably circled around them were all that he'd told himself he wanted nothing to do with. His mother had secrets. Bernard and the other Senior Donovans had kept secrets. Those secrets had ended with emotional and physical pain, disenchantment and anger. It had impacted two generations of Donovans and ended the lives of many others who really had nothing to do with the affair between Roslyn and Henry Donovan which had led to all the turmoil in the first place. No, Dane thought as he opened the door to his room and walked inside, he was not about to travel down that path for a woman he barely knew.

Even if she had been originally running from some type of domestic situation, why sleep with Emmet? And him? Dane didn't have the answers, but his irritation about the situation was rising, to a point where he didn't care about the answers, he just wanted to get out as unscathed as he possibly could.

He dropped his bag by the door and headed into the

bedroom where he stripped his clothes off and went into the bathroom to shower. Afterwards, he dressed in jeans and a polo shirt. Dane had no idea where Zera was, but he planned to have her bags and all her belongings packed and ready for her to pick up whenever she returned. He'd just put on his shoes and was about to grab Zera's duffel bag off the floor, when he heard the knock at the door.

Not in the mood for any interruptions, Dane considered ignoring the knock. But before he could decide, it sounded again, this time louder. Fists clenching at his sides he stalked out of the bedroom and into the main sitting area of the room. He was almost to the door when the knock came again. Dane grabbed the handle and yanked the door open, ready to curse whoever was on the other side.

"We've got a problem," Roark said, effectively silencing Dane's planned tirade.

Before Dane could even figure out a retort, Roark was walking into the room. He wore dark blue jeans today—a first since each time Dane had seen him, his cousin had been wearing a suit—and a light blue shirt. When Dane closed the door and turned to ask what was going on, he saw Roark pulling his cell phone from his back pocket.

"What's going on?" Dane asked him. "Is there a problem at the new building? Did one of the background checks we were waiting on turn up something bad?"

Roark's thick eyebrows were drawn as he frowned and punched a number into his phone before placing the call on speaker.

"Just a sec," Roark said to Dane. "Hopefully this will make more sense coming from him."

Who was "him"?

Dane was past fed up with not knowing what was happening around him. Just a month ago he'd told himself he was finally in control of his life again. He had no loose ends—namely his mother and sister—that he had to tend do. All the crazy and unpredictability was over. At least that's what he'd thought.

"Hey," another male voice replied when the ringing of the phone stopped.

"Yeah," Roark said. "I'm here. Tell him what you just told me."

Another "him". Dane's frown was beginning to give him a headache. He stepped closer to where Roark was now standing near the couch holding the phone between them.

"Who is this? Tell me what's going on."

"It's me, Cade," the voice on the phone stated. "You wanna tell us why your name just showed up in official FBI documents?"

Special Agent Cadence "Cade" Donovan was the son of Charles and Brenda Donovan who lived in Arlington, Virginia. Charles had followed in his father, Cephus's, footsteps and ran a commercial division of Donovan Oilwell. Cade had one sister named, Dakota.

Dane folded his arms over his chest as the rest of what he'd learned about this particular Donovan circled in his mind. Cade was an FBI profiler who had assisted in profiling Dane's mother when Roslyn's many crimes took a national turn.

"What are you talking about?" Dane asked.

Roark was still scowling and Dane was starting to think it was a favored Donovan facial expression.

"My unit was asked to look at some files that the organized crime unit compiled for an international case they'd been working on. Imagine my surprise when not only does my cousin's name pop up in some of the reports, but surveillance pictures of him surfaced along with questions about whether or not an official inquiry needs to be opened on him, his businesses and his family. An official inquiry that would undoubtedly lead to me being taken off this case and possibly investigated for organized crime connections as well," Cade said.

The irritated tone in his voice was nothing compared to the fury roiling through Dane at this moment.

"Tell me everything," Dane said.

"No. How about you start by telling us everything," Roark insisted.

Dane didn't budge. "I don't have anything to tell you."

"You sure? Because you and this woman in the pictures look really comfy and cozy on this yacht. And again at a restaurant at your hotel, and then, this pic that's a bit blurry, but pretty much tells what was happening on this table in your hotel room. It looks like you have a lot to tell us," Cade said.

"Why?" Dane asked. "Who is she?"

Because Dane knew for certain he had no connections to organized crime. So his line of thought immediately went to Zera. Who the hell was she affiliated with that would put him in this position?

Cade chuckled. "Oh yeah, that's the best part of this," he said.

Dane didn't think there was a "best part" to whatever was happening now. It couldn't be.

"Zera Kennedy is also a special agent for the FBI. At least she was until about four and a half years ago when she took a leave of absence from the Intelligence Department where she was working in D.C."

Zera was FBI?

Dane let his arms fall to his sides. He walked to the window and stood there, staring out at the city. He probably should keep the drapes drawn since he now knew he was being watched.

"Zera Kennedy is a woman that I met four years ago when I was in Paris on business," Dane said. "I bumped into her again when I returned, ten days ago."

"And you've had nothing to do with her in between that time? You never talked to her, wrote to her? Nothing?" Cade asked.

"There was no contact after I left four years ago. And the meeting this time was not planned. It was purely by chance," Dane said.

But now, he had to wonder.

"So this Zera Kennedy is working on a case here in Paris?" Roark asked. "I didn't think the FBI took international cases."

"We can liaison with international agencies," Cade said. "But there's no paperwork that officially assigned Zera to any case. I was going to reach out to her former unit to see if anyone knew why she'd left and how a leave of absence could be extended for so long. But I needed to clean the mess in my backyard first."

"There is no mess," Dane stated. "I did not know she was FBI. I don't know what she's doing here. I don't even know where she lives."

"Apparently she lives with you," Cade quipped.

Dane turned to face Roark who had set the cell phone on the table and was now dragging a hand down his face.

"She's been staying here for the past five days. I don't know why," Dane said and then shook his head. "Except for the obvious, I don't know why she left the place where she had been staying. I know next to nothing about her which is why I asked Bailey—"

"What? Wait? You opened a private investigation into an FBI agent?" Roark asked.

"And you asked Bailey, our newly married, was just kidnapped almost a year ago cousin, to help you? Are you crazy? The Seniors are going to want to kill you for this, Dane! Uncle Albert will be first in line. What were you thinking?" Cade asked.

"I was thinking that for once I could turn to family for help and that wouldn't be such a bad thing," Dane said before he could think better of it.

It had been his intention to never show these people, or anyone else, any weakness. No vulnerabilities. No weak points in which they could use to infiltrate and break him. Ever. It was how he'd been forced to act all his life. People liked to say that no man was an island, well, Dane sure was. He'd had to be, or he would have been sucked in by his mother and his sister's madness. Standing alone meant he only ever had to apologize to himself.

"Look," he said when the room remained silent after his outburst. "She's just someone I've been sleeping with. Nothing more. Besides, I'm scheduled to leave in a couple of days."

Actually, Dane thought he might be leaving Paris sooner.

"In the meantime, I can simply send her on her way. I'll be out of your investigation file. Case closed," Dane finished.

"Are you in love with her?" Roark asked.

Dane looked at him incredulously. "What? No! Like I said, we've just been sleeping together. Sex. That's all."

Roark didn't look as if he believed him.

"How bad is it, Cade?" Roark asked.

"Well, I can't touch it, that's for sure," Cade told them. "I'll give my partner the low down and let him prepare a report. He'll have to submit that report to the Director, with a signed statement from you Dane. Then I think it'll blow over. As long as there are no further connections."

"There will be none," Dane stated firmly. "She'll be out of this room this evening. And I will be back in the States before the end of the week."

"Do me a favor and make a pit stop at Quantico so we can get this all resolved, nice and neatly," Cade told him.

"That's fine," Dane said. "I'll let you know when I'm on my way."

"Good. Now, I gotta go because it looks like whatever Agent Kennedy has been doing while she's been in Paris, is about to take a bad turn," Cade said before disconnecting the call.

Dane refused to be bothered by his cousin's parting words.

Roark reached for his phone and pressed the button to clear his screen. He sat down heavily on the couch and stared at Dane.

"We're not used to this type of drama," Roark said. "I know we're part of the Donovan family, but we're relatively low key here in the UK."

Dane took a seat in one of the chairs by the window. "There is nothing low key about any of the Donovans."

Roark shrugged. "Yourself included."

"It's not what I wanted," Dane said. He leaned forward and rested his elbows on his knees.

Roark chuckled. "In my thirty-six years, I've never known a person to get only the things they wanted."

Dane had to smirk at the truth in that remark.

CHAPTER 10

*P*ierre Newton was the fourth name on the tenth page of the agenda book that Zera had taken from Emmet's safe. When she decided that it was time to approach him, Zera had no idea that he would be the photographer taking pictures of Ines.

She was gorgeous. Her hair had been teased so that she had that "I just had great sex" look. Her eyes were perfectly smoky, her lips coated with red matte lipstick that added an inviable fullness to her mouth. Even though Zera was mighty proud of her own medium-thick lips. Ines had a fresh, effortlessly sexy look that Zera knew appealed to photographers and fashion houses. New clothing designs were only partially about the actual clothes. The rest was how well a fabulous model would actually make the clothes look. As she watched Ines pose, pout, smile, glower and even pucker on command, Zera, once again, confirmed that Ines was only one picture away from bursting onto the modeling scene.

And Pierre Newton might just be the one to get her there.

He was a phenomenal photographer. Unfortunately, he was also a drug dealer who was mixed up with an organization that was far more dangerous than Zera suspected he knew. She'd been following up on information about Pierre for the past week, since she'd been chased. That meant she was getting close. Hacking into the cell provider's network was easy. Downloading Pierre's call record was enlightening. He was in touch with Luka Kuznetsov, Emmet's UK contact.

Luka Kuznetsov was part of the illusive Belyakov *bratva*, the Russian crime family that Zera was certain had orchestrated Hiari's and who knew how many other kidnappings in Africa and other countries. He was the man she wanted. The one she would make tell her where her cousin was.

"Hey! I did not know you were coming to see me today!" Ines yelled exuberantly as she came over to where Zera was standing.

Zera hugged her friend and tried to pretend like this was a planned visit—one where she had actually come to see Ines.

"Hey. Yeah, I um, was in the area and thought I'd drop in and say hello," she said.

"Oh? I did not realize I even told you about tonight's shoot," Ines said.

Zera sighed inwardly, but kept her smile in place.

"But we can leave and go grab some dinner. I'm starving," Ines suggested.

"Sure. Let's do that. Don't you have to change first?" Zera asked. She looked down at the flowing ice blue gown Ines was wearing.

Thin straps held the dress on her shoulders while the neckline plunged to show an expanse of her creamy white skin. Her small breasts were hidden by the material, but the fact that she wore no bra was made apparent by the sharp peaks of her nipples through the material.

"Of course," Ines said with a giggle. "I'll go clean my face too and grab my things. Be back in ten."

"I'll be right here," Zera said because she knew that Ines would only take ten minutes to change.

When Ines had disappeared through a scarred brown door, Zera crossed the room. They were in an old warehouse with high ceilings and one long white wall. The floor in front of the wall was white as well and it was where Ines had been standing as she posed for the pictures. Props, Zera thought as she crossed it to get to the area where two camera stands were positioned and Pierre stood with his back to her. He was staring down at the camera he held in his hand.

"It's lovely that you have this little side business," Zera said as she came up behind him.

He turned his head slowly, glancing at her dismissively over his shoulder.

"Did Cara send you?" he asked before turning to look at his camera again. "I don't need another girl."

"Really? What would Luka have to say about you turning away possible workers?"

She knew the name she'd just dropped would get his attention.

Pierre turned to her, still moving slowly, as if he had all the time in the world. Zera figured that was true. She wasn't here to arrest him. She couldn't even if she wanted to. While she had sufficient evidence, she wasn't here in the official capacity of a law enforcement agent. She was rogue. She had been for almost five years and while she knew that one act may have effectively ended her career with the FBI, she didn't care. She'd had to do it. Her family was depending on her.

He stepped close to her and Zera simply lifted her chin so that she could hold eye contact. Pierre was a slim man, just a bit over six feet tall, his brown hair a scraggly mess, his beard splotchy and in need of a trim.

"You'd better watch your mouth, *petite fille*," he said.

Then his hand was plastered to the back of her head as he pulled her closer to him. It was a quick move, one Zera hadn't anticipated. But she'd slipped her gun from the back ban of her jeans and pressed it into his stomach, just as fast.

"No. How about you tell me where I can find Luka and I let you live," she told him.

He smiled. His hand slipping slowly from her head as he took a step back. Zera followed, keeping the gun on him.

"I know he's looking for me. I want to make his hunt a little easier. Tell me where he is, Pierre, or the police will hear about your other business—the shipment and distribution one that pays directly to Luka."

Everything Zera had on Pierre was already carefully documented in a file on a USB drive that she kept in a safe at the bank. She updated the files weekly while sitting at her museum of choice. Aasir knew about the safe and so did her mother, or rather she'd written a letter explaining everything to her mother and her grandmother and had made Aasir swear to give it to them if anything should happen to her. Her finger tightened on the trigger as she decided nothing was going to happen to her and she was getting Hiari back.

"He will kill you, black bitch!" Pierre spat. "First he will use you and then he will kill you!"

Zera raised her arm until the gun was pointing directly at Pierre's head.

"Not before I splatter your brains all over this nice pristine floor. Now tell me where I can find Luka."

Pierre laughed and then shrugged. "Sure. Why not? It is your death. Not mine. He is at The Grande."

"Zera?" Ines called from behind.

Zera didn't turn immediately, but stepped closer to Pierre and smacked him hard with her gun. He dropped instantly and Zera moved fast dropping her backpack to the floor and pulling the zipper open.

"What are you doing? What's happened?" Ines was asking.

She'd come close enough so that Zera could see her but Zera did not stop. She pulled out a small red stress ball, stuffing it into Pierre's mouth. Then she found her electrical tape, applying three layers over his mouth stretching it from ear-to-ear. Next she bound his hands, pulling so tight she knew the rope would cut deep into his skin each time he moved. His ankles were also bound and when she stood, she kicked him in the balls and the stomach. Pierre may not have known where Hiari was taken, but he was a part of the crew that did. Zera had a timeline and a list of possible places the group of girls Hiari had been with were taken. Their group had been called The Pir, or The Feast in Russian. Zera planned to make a feast out of Luka and his *pakhan*, boss, when she found them.

But right now, she had to deal with Ines.

"Wait, you are an American FBI agent? But you are here in Paris? Why?" Ines asked as they stepped out of the taxi.

She had been talking constantly after she insisted she was

going with Zera when they left the warehouse. Zera had momentarily considered tying her up and gagging her too, but she hadn't wanted to scar Ines in any way. Nor did she want to scare her any more than she knew she already had.

"Look, it is a long story, Ines. One I do not want you unnecessarily involved in," Zera said.

She paid for the taxi and stepped out onto a dark street.

"Why don't you take the taxi and go home. Or better, take a holiday with your grandmother. She'll love that. She adores the beach."

Ines shook her head. "Do not try to brush me off. I want to know what is happening. You never told me any of this and I have known you for months now. Are you in trouble?"

"No," Zera replied instantly as she stepped onto the sidewalk and looked up at the white twinkling lights that spelled out The Grande.

She had no back up and only her gun and knife at her ankle. She was acting on information that only she knew, in an area of the 18th Arrondissement that she had done no research on. She'd simply acted because she felt like her time to do so was running out. All because she'd slept with Dane again. She shouldn't have and she knew it, but she had and now she suspected her feelings were involved. None of that could be if she did not complete her task. She had to focus.

"I have to go in here and speak to someone. Why don't you wait out here for me?" she asked, hoping Ines would agree with her.

"Absolutely not!" was Ines's response.

Ines had changed into white leggings and a long white tank top. Her shoes were fuchsia sandals and her hair was now pulled back into a messy bun.

"I'm going with you in case something happens."

Zera shook her head. "And what are you going to do if something does happen, Ines? This isn't your fight. You should go home."

"You said someone kidnapped your cousin. Well, I consider you my family. So that makes this my business."

"This is not a game!" Zera yelled and instantly regretted it.

"I'm not letting you go in alone. If things get bad I'm calling the police. Now come on, let's get this over with."

Zera sighed heavily. Her options now were to walk away and take Ines home, or to go forward. Was she really ready to approach Luka? Hell yes! She had proof that Emmet had been the Belyakov *bratva's* contact for the African region. So she'd gotten close to him and when the time had availed itself she'd taken Emmet's agenda book which had everything she needed to know to move forward. There were dozens of groups named with dates beside them. The dates of when they were taken and from what region. That's how she'd known which group Hiari had been in. Emmet was very detailed—she suspected so that he would have some assurance for himself—so he also had notes regarding where the groups would be taken and how much he had been paid for them. Everything was in that book. Everything except the last stop for The Pir group, the group that Hiari was in.

Now, she was here. She could get in Luka's face and demand a meeting with his *pakhan*. From there she would use Emmet's book to negotiate Hiari's safe return. And once she had Hiari out safely, she would send her copy of the book to the local police and every other national agency that were supposed to be searching for leads to stop the kidnappings and human trafficking around the world.

"Are you coming?" Ines asked.

Zera looked up to see that she had moved closer to the door and already had her hand on the handle. Ines pulled the door open and walked inside without waiting for Zera's answer. Cursing, Zera went in behind her.

The inside of The Grande was dark, the jazzy sounds of a trumpet and saxophone echoed from further inside, to the front entrance. They walked through a stone archway and Zera took note of the two burly white men standing on either side. The looks they gave Zera and Ines were cold and assessing, but Ines flashed her brilliant smile and glanced back at Zera. Sighing because there was no going back now, Zera reached into her pocket and pulled out a stack of euros. The amount was probably somewhere around one hundred US dollars. She held it between her fingers and arched a brow as she waited to see if one of the goons would take it.

The one on the left gave a dismissive shrug, while the guy on the right, with the jagged pink scar beneath his left eye looked Ines up and down appreciatively. When he turned his attention to Zera, the appreciation continued and he actually smiled as he took the money from her. Zera tried not to cringe as they walked further into the club, knowing that Scarface was most likely still staring at them.

The place was filled with people sitting at round tables made to accommodate two. Red cushioned chairs were positioned at each. Along a back wall were red plush benches with longer square tables in front of them. To the far left was a bar, with the wall full of bottles of liquor lined neatly and illuminated by a hazy red light. A stage stretched across the front of the room. It was curved to allow a good view from any angle. In a dark corner, near the only Exit door Zera could find, was a glossy black piano. A slim black man sat at the piano and played without ever looking up to the crowd. While the saxophone and trumpet players, both white, stood to one side of the piano and played along.

"Do you see him?" Ines asked.

Zera shook her head. The pictures Aasir was able to send her of Luka Kuznetsov had not been great. His features had been grainy at best, so picking him out in this dark club wasn't going to be easy. But she knew how to get his attention.

"Let's sit at the bar," she said and walked in that direction.

When they'd ordered drinks and sat waiting for them, Zera decided that she did need to at least let someone know where she was. She pulled out her cell phone to send a message to Aasir. Since this was her real phone, she would send the message to an email box that was registered to a library in Kenya. Aasir had created the mailbox and would be the only one checking the messages. Just as she sent the message letting him know that she'd seen Pierre and was now at the club looking for Luka, a text message came through.

WE NEED TO TALK

It was from Dane.

It was a little after seven in the evening and Zera hadn't been back to the hotel all day. She'd slipped out this morning before he could wake because she'd needed to finally take care of her business. But she hadn't left him a note and so he was probably worried about her. But "we need to talk" did not sound like he was worried. It sounded like he was fed up. With a heavy sigh, Zera put the phone back into her pocket. She picked up the glass that the bartender had just set in front of her and she drank the whiskey. It burned her throat so much her eyes watered, but she shook it off. Just in time to see Scarface from the front door approaching them.

"Come with me," he said stiffly, his thick Russian accent undeniable.

"Stay here," Zera told Ines.

"No. Both. Come with me," he said adamantly and then turned, expecting them to follow.

Zera did not want to go with Ines.

"Go out the exit door," she said quietly as she slipped off the seat. "Now!"

"No. I'm not leaving you," Ines insisted.

She got off her seat and walked ahead of Zera once more. Zera gritted her teeth and swore she was going to shake the hell out of Ines for being so stubborn once they got home. *If*, they got home, was Zera's next thought. Because as they walked through the club, two more men came up behind them while Scarface led them toward a black door that blended in with the black wall.

Seconds after Scarface walked through the door, he turned, grabbing Ines around the waist and pulling her back up against him.

"Shit!" Zera cursed and reached for her gun.

One of the men behind her hit Zera across her shoulders with something and she fell, her gun sliding across the floor.

"Get her!" Scarface yelled. "Bring them both to the truck!"

"Not today!" Zera replied.

She rolled over onto her back at exactly the moment that one of the other burly guys came for her.

"Get up, bitch!" he yelled and bent lower to pick her up.

Zera lifted her leg, pulled her knife and sliced both his arms before he could touch her. He flailed backward yelling out in pain. The other guy was coming for her. Zera jumped to her feet. These guys were big but they weren't light on their feet, so Zera was able to dodge to the side and then go in, jabbing the knife into the other guy's side. She made the colossal mistake of thinking that made her the winner, but when she turned it was to see Scarface tossing Ines to the floor like a ragdoll. He aimed his gun at her. Zera spotted her gun on the floor, behind him.

"Hey!" Ines yelled.

She'd picked up Zera's gun.

"Ines, no!" Zera screamed, but it was too late.

Scarface had turned quickly firing at Ines. She took the bullet and slammed into the wall. Zera screamed. She jumped onto Scarface's back, sinking her knife into his skin a few inches from his spine. He yelled in Russian, calling her all kinds of names, but Zera held onto him, pulling her knife out and jabbing it back into him again. Scarface turned, slamming her back to the wall, temporarily knocking the wind out of her. But Zera didn't have time to be hurt. She scrambled across the floor while Scarface was staggering, his wounds bleeding profusely. She got to her gun, lifted it and shot him where he stood.

When Scarface fell, the other two, whom Zera suspected did not have guns, scattered, shouting "Backup! Backup!" into the radio pieces they wore at their ears.

"Dammit!" Zera was cursing again.

She went to Ines whose chest was covered in blood, her eyes wide, pupils dilated.

"You are gonna be just fine," she told her. "Silly girl. I told you to go home."

Zera lifted Ines's arm and quickly wrapped it around her neck. She stood, pulling Ines up with her and dragged her friend with her to the door they'd come through. This hallway apparently wasn't soundproof so in the main area of the club pandemonium had ensued at the sound of the gunshots. People were running and screaming, trying to get to either the exit door or the entrance. Zera spotted more goon-like men coming from the exit toward where she was standing. She ducked her head down and tightened her grip around Ines's waist.

Moving with the crowd and praying none of Luka's men could see her, Zera continued to move. Her gun in one hand, the other hand feeling the blood that had seeped through Ines's blouse, warm her fingers. They made it to the front door and the sound of sirens was a godsend. But Zera knew that until she was in a police cruiser, she and Ines were still in danger. So she moved down toward the end of the block, away from the crowd.

"I've got you," she told Ines as she lowered her to the ground and propped her up on the wall. "We're gonna get you to a hospital and they're gonna fix you right up."

Ines was not talking and her lids had lowered.

"No. No. No. You look at me, Ines. Look at me!" Zera insisted.

Ines did not open her eyes. Zera's heart slammed against her chest and her other hand continued to grip the gun as she looked down toward the club. People were pouring out, those goons included. They had looked up the street in her direction, but she'd pushed Ines back into the doorway of a storefront. It was dark up here, they wouldn't see her. Hopefully.

Police cars pulled up from different directions. The one that came down the side of the street where they were became Zera's savior. She leapt up from where she'd been crouched and ran out into the street, waving for the officer to stop. He did, and jumped out of the vehicle.

"She's shot!" Zera told him. "My friend. Right over here! She's been shot!"

"*Où? Nous avons besoin d'une ambulance! Tout de suite!*" the officer yelled into his radio.

"Yes! Yes! An ambulance! Yes!" Zera repeated over and over again. That's just what they needed an ambulance because Ines was going to be fine. She was going to get up and give Zera her brilliant smile. She was going to walk down the runway in the Paris Fashion Week and she was going to be fabulous. She had to.

Zera's hands were shaking when the ambulance finally arrived. It wasn't until she'd climbed into the back of the ambulance that she realized at some point after the officer had arrived, she'd dropped her gun. It didn't matter. Only Ines mattered. Tears stung her eyes and Zera shook her head. Ines mattered. Her life. Her career. It mattered. Zera would never forgive herself if she'd done something to end that. She couldn't take it. First Hiari and now Ines. No, she thought as one tear rolled down her face regardless of how a part of her knew it was futile. It could not be Ines.

The ringing of her cell phone scared her and Zera hurriedly wiped the tears from her eyes as if she thought whoever was calling her would see them. She felt like crying all over again when she looked down at her hands and saw the blood. Ines's blood.

"Hello," she answered, her voice shaking just like her hands.

"Zera?"

It was Dane.

"We need to talk. I've been trying to reach you all day. It's important that we talk tonight. I'm leaving in the morning."

He was saying something. A lot of something but Zera just wasn't deciphering it all.

"My friend's been shot," she said. "She's bleeding. We're in an ambulance and she might…she's…I can't talk to you right now." She disconnected the call and returned her attention to Ines.

This was no time for distractions.

Had Dane said he was leaving tomorrow?

PART II

Rain can soak a leopard's skin but it does not wash out its spots.

—*African Proverb*

CHAPTER 11

*D*ane was a fool.

He knew this and still drove to the hospital in search of Zera and her friend.

It had been the way she sounded when she'd answered the phone. Shaken, was the best way to describe it. Dane hadn't liked that sound. He was already packed, his suitcases in the trunk of the car. All he had to do was drive to the San Régis where he planned to spend tonight. His jet would be here first thing tomorrow morning to take him back to New York. There had really been no need to speak to Zera personally. He could have simply sent her a text letting her know that he'd paid for the room at the Novotel through the early part of next week, so she could stay there if she needed to.

Why should she need a place to stay? If she was an American agent working on some type of case, wouldn't her lodging be taken care of? But Cade said she was on a leave of absence? So what was she doing? Cade had also mentioned an organized crime case. Was Zera involved with the mafia in some way?

It didn't matter, Dane told himself as he parked the car and prepared to get out. None of this mattered to him. He did not live in Paris and he and Zera were not involved in a relationship. It was an affair, just as they had shared before. Nothing new here. Except that he had gotten out of the car and was now entering the building. He had no idea where he was going, but once in the emergency department he saw a cluster of police officers and figured that was a good place to start.

Zera said her friend was shot. That was a crime, so police should be involved. Dane tapped one of the officers on the shoulder and told him who he was looking for. At first the man had looked clueless, but then another officer standing behind him said, "Down that hall. In the first examining room. The detectives are in there with her."

He'd spoken in French while eyeing Dane as if he wanted him to explain who he was and why he was there. But Dane didn't say another word to him. Instead he walked down the hall the way the officer had indicated and made a left turn into the first exam room. He stopped just inside the door when he saw her.

There was blood on her face and her hands. Her shirt and the left upper half of her jeans were soaked in blood. Dane's fists clenched at his side and he told himself to remain calm. She was sitting up on the side of a bed, while a nurse unwrapped a blood pressure cuff from her arm.

"What else did you see?" a man dressed in a dark wrinkled blue suit asked in French.

"It was dark," Zera said. "People were running and

screaming and we were just trying to get out. I had to kind of carry Ines because she was shot and she was bleeding so much."

"But you did not get shot," the man asked her. He wore wire-rimmed glasses pushed high on his face. His silver hair was parted and slicked down on the sides. He held a pencil and notepad but wasn't writing anything down. "Where was your friend when she was shot?"

Zera blinked. The nurse took advantage of Zera's momentary silence by placing a thermometer into her mouth. Zera continued blinking while the officer stared at her. When the thermometer beeped the nurse took it out of Zera's mouth and wrote something on a piece of paper.

"Miss…you never gave me your last name," the man said to Zera.

"Kennedy," she replied. "My name is Zera Kennedy."

Up to this point the entire exchange had been in French, but when Zera said her name she'd spoken clear and concise English, without her African accent.

It occurred to Dane in that moment that there'd been another time that he'd heard Zera speak this way. At Emmet's New Year's Eve party. She looked beautiful that night, sexy and alluring. But no one would have ever guessed she was a native African.

"Were you standing near your friend when she was shot? Did you see who shot her?"

Zera blinked again and as if she just realized he was there, her gaze found Dane's.

The nurse said something about x-rays and needing to get her out of those clothes and the man frowned.

"I will be right outside," he told her.

Dane did not move when the man passed him and walked

through the open door. The nurse looked at Dane and was about to say something but Zera spoke.

"You came," she whispered. "I didn't mean for you...I mean, I didn't tell you to."

"There's a lot of things you didn't tell me, Zera," Dane said.

She turned to look at the nurse. "Can you leave us alone? I mean, don't you have to go somewhere to schedule the x-rays or whatever you insist on doing to me?"

The nurse continued to stare at Dane. When Zera spoke again, this time her voice slightly elevated, repeating her request, the nurse jumped and tore her gaze away from him.

"*Oui. Oui. Je reviens tout de suite,*" the nurse said.

The nurse moved away from the bed, announcing that she would be right back before walking past Dane slowly until she was out the door. Dane immediately moved behind the nurse and closed the door.

"What happened?" he asked when they were alone.

She took a deep breath and exhaled. "We were at a club having drinks and someone started shooting."

That was a lie, or at least it wasn't the total truth. Dane was sure of it.

"Just a random shooting," he continued.

He considered crossing the room to stand closer to her. To touch her and assure himself that she was not physically wounded. He did not move.

"Was anyone besides your friend shot?" he asked.

Zera started to shake her head, and then she shrugged. "I don't know. I was only concerned about Ines."

"Did they catch the shooter?"

For an instant her eyes grew wider, hopeful. But that look

was quickly dashed as she stared down at her hands and sighed. "I don't know."

"Did you see the shooter?"

She hesitated before shaking her head.

"Did you know the shooter, Special Agent Kennedy? Maybe he was someone you were investigating who didn't want to be found," he said and waited for her response.

Zera lifted her head very slowly. She looked at him through narrowed eyes and moved her arms to drag her fingers through her tangled hair.

"How did you find out?" she asked. "Because if there's someone out there that knows, that could explain why I was chased through the streets last week."

Dane watched as she talked. She didn't look upset, not at the fact that he'd found out her secret. But she did look irritated at the thought that other people, besides him, knew who she really was.

"That's when you came to me, wasn't it? The night someone chased you on the streets? You think they knew who you were? Did you speak to them with your natural accent, or did you lose it the way you just did with that cop? The way you did at Emmet's party?"

"You don't understand," she started to say.

He interrupted. "Explain it to me. All of it."

Zera jumped down from the bed. She lifted the blood soaked shirt up and over her head, dropping it into the tall trash can in the corner. On the bed beside where she'd been sitting was a paper blue robe folded into a square. She picked it up, unfolded it and put her arms through the holes on the side. She stripped off her pants and shoes, then walked over to the small sink in the corner and washed her hands and face. She pulled towels from the box on the wall and turned back to face him. Her arms hung at her sides, then she folded them across her chest, the blue gown crackling with her every motion.

"I was with the FBI and now I'm not. I left," she said with a huff. "I left because my cousin was kidnapped and I needed to find her. My family needs me to find her."

"So you left your job in law enforcement to what, work on your own? That doesn't make sense, Zera. Why wouldn't you stay at work and use the resources you most likely had at your disposal? And why come here and start sleeping with Emmet? How did that help in your supposed investigation?"

"I," she started to say, but stopped. "I don't expect you to understand my reasons. I don't expect anyone too. But that is the truth. I took a leave of absence because I knew that looking for Hiari was out of the FBI's jurisdiction."

"And yet here you are." Dane shook his head. "And Emmet?" He brought it up again, not because he was jealous. He was not. But because he needed all these pieces that had been floating around in his mind to finally fit.

She squared her shoulders. "Emmet was a means to an end. I needed to get close to him to get closer to the people I suspected of taking Hiari. I didn't speak naturally in front of him because I didn't want him to know where I came from, or to have any reason to ask."

"Is that why you slept with him? So you could get information from him?" Dane asked but he wasn't certain he was going to believe what she had to say. He couldn't believe anything she said anymore. That bothered him way more than Dane wanted it to.

"I did not sleep with Emmet Parks," Zera stated evenly. "I know you don't believe me, but there it is. Emmet was impotent.

His doctor said it was more of a mental issue than a physical one, but either way, he couldn't get it up. Ever. So instead," she paused and took another deep breath. "He liked to watch me pleasure myself. That got him off."

Dane clenched his teeth. His fists balled at his sides and he wanted to hit something. The thought of her...in front of Emmet, or anyone for that matter...just picturing it in his mind. He shook his head.

"You let me believe differently. He introduced you as his woman. You didn't try to stop me to tell me." And Dane realized now that he really wished she had done just that.

"I had a job to do," she said. "I never meant to lie to you or to—"

"Stop," Dane told her and held his hand up just in case his command wasn't enough. "I don't need to hear anymore. Look, I'm sorry about your friend being shot. But I'm glad you're okay."

"Dane," she said.

He shook his head and continued, "I've paid for the hotel room until next Tuesday. Stay until then if you want to. I'm leaving tomorrow."

She crossed the room and stopped in front of him. "I did not sleep with Emmet. The time we spent together was probably the best time of my adult life. If I thought there was a way I could have told you and still gotten the information I needed, I would have done it."

"Fine!" Dane yelled. "It's all fine now. It happened. It's done. I'm leaving."

He felt like he'd just said that, but that he needed to say it again, and again, to prove that he was actually doing it.

"Dane," she whispered and reached up to touch his arm.

Dane pulled away. "Look, I've had enough of lies and deceit with the façade of good intentions behind them. I'm not going through it again. If you say you have a job to do, then by all means, do it, Zera. This affair, this *last* affair, is over."

Dane moved quickly then, moving to the door and wrenching it open. He walked through it fast and pushed past the two officers who were standing right outside the room. One called out to him and Dane counted himself lucky that his walking away didn't end with him being shot in the back. He stalked out of the hospital and through the parking lot, not letting go of the breath he'd been holding since walking away from her, until he was in his car, his forehead resting on the steering wheel.

What was he supposed to do now?

Zera's chest hurt, but as the technician explained after her x-rays were complete, there were no cracked ribs or other injuries that could be seen on the scan. To be fair, her shoulder blades hurt as well. The doctor who examined her said there was a violent bruise that would cause her pain for the next few days or until all the bruising went away. But that overall she'd been lucky not to sustain any gunshot wounds.

He was right about that, even though Zera was almost willing to admit the pain she was feeling right now might be comparable to being shot. It was ridiculous and yet, she'd known from the moment she'd seen him at the museum that this was going to happen. Four years ago she'd been well on her way to falling in love with Dane. His leaving had actually saved her from a fate that she wouldn't have known how to deal with. Now, Zera still had no idea what to do with all these feelings that were jumbled in her chest causing the ball of pain. Especially now that Dane had left once again.

She had no idea how to analyze what was happening. How had Dane found out who she really was? And why had he looked so angry, and just as hurt, by that news? They were having an affair. Zera knew that. Just because she knew she had more feelings for Dane than an affair would allow, didn't mean she couldn't understand the rules. And Dane's rules hadn't change. At least he'd never mentioned them changing. So maybe it was just anger that she'd seen in his eyes and the way he'd stood stiffly as if moving may have somehow worsened the situation.

What did any of it matter now? Dane was gone, or he would be in the morning. He'd said she could stay at the hotel until next week and that's what Zera had decided to do. She definitely could not go back to her apartment. She would call Ines's grandmother after she'd had a chance to see Ines, so that she could report the entire situation accurately. Or at least as accurately as would be allowed under the circumstances. She had just stepped off the elevator and turned down the hallway toward the numbered rooms where Ines had been taken after her surgery, when a hand grabbed her arm tightly, pulling her inside of a small room.

Zera yanked her arm free and spun around instantly, fists clenched and drawn, prepared to fight. She'd lost her gun and her knife in the chaos at the club, but she still had significant hand-to-hand combat from her training at The Academy.

"I told you to get someplace safe," Necole LeAmbette said after she'd closed the door.

Zera let her arms fall to her side and stood up straight. She took a quick breath and shook her head. "I did," she replied.

Necole tilted her head and raised one beautifully arched brow. "I can't tell."

Necole was born in Nigeria, but moved to London with her parents when she was three years old. She was also married to a French policeman. When Aasir first told Zera about the kidnapping and gave her Debare Adebayo's name as a possible suspect, he'd quickly realized that Zera planned to go after Debare on her own. And since neither of them were in a position to go off investigating international crimes, Aasir linked Zera to Necole, an Interpol agent. But after their first meeting that took place just a few weeks after Zera arrived in Paris, Necole had made it perfectly clear that the case belonged to her and the joint task force which had been put in place by four of the countries plagued by kidnappings involving Foreign Terrorist Organizations. In short, she'd told Zera to go back to her job in the States. Zera hadn't listened because she knew that Necole's task force could only collect information, it was still up to the separate countries to apprehend and prosecute the offenders. And, as Zera had just reminded Aasir, those countries weren't doing anything.

"Aasir told me you had not left," Necole continued.

She wore a black pantsuit, her platform-heeled pumps adding another four inches to her normal five foot eleven stature. Her hair was long and wavy, make-up perfectly done. She did not look like an Interpol agent, but more like a movie star.

"I told him that was unwise. Then you called me," Necole said.

"They came after me," Zera interrupted. "I had to call you

because I'm not authorized to make any arrests. I had a license plate that I was going to give to you so that you could run it."

"That was not necessary," Necole said. "Abram Goraya and Evgeni Dyogtin, two of the three men you injured at The Grande tonight. They are former spies from the Belyakov *bratva* working their way up in the organization. Abram was positioned at your apartment last week. Edouard Dubois was the one who chased you at the museum. He's an associate on loan from another organization, but Misha is growing weary of him, especially since he lost you on the street and Evgeni was forced to pick up our trail at the garage."

Zera tried not to be amazed and irritated at the same time. Not only did Necole know all the players that Zera had just learned about in the last five months, but she also knew where they were as if she'd been watching them, while they watched Zera.

"Why were they chasing me?" she asked.

Necole leaned against a cart and crossed one ankle over the other.

"You have something they're threatened by. Either that or Emmet told you something they want to know. I haven't figured out which one yet, since you blatantly disregarded my directive to leave the country. As soon as our intelligence picked up your name from our surveillance, I knew we had to get eyes on you too."

Zera ignored the obvious ire in Necole's voice. Zera didn't work for Interpol. As a matter of fact, she wasn't technically working for anyone at this point. Therefore, Necole had no authority over her.

"I stayed as a visitor to this city. There was no reason for you to make me leave."

Necole shook her head. "You were sleeping with Emmet Parks who was in charge of the African Region of the Belyakov *bratva's* empire. That's not something I would call a romantic love affair. I knew what you were doing all along."

"And you let me do all the legwork, so you can now come in and take over," Zera spat. "Not a chance."

She attempted to walk past but Necole grabbed her by the arm.

"You will walk away now, Zera. Or I'll call your Director and tell him what you've been up to. I'd hate to ruin what could become a brilliant career. But you really need to walk away now. Go back to your job, explain that you had some type of work relapse or something. Sit in that office and find the intelligence they need to put more criminals away in the United States. But do not think about this case again. Misha Belyakov and the empire his father built and nurtured for more than fifty years, is out of your league," Necole told her.

Again, Zera pulled her arm away. "Don't touch me again," Zera stated through clenched teeth. "And I'm not leaving Paris until I find out where Hiari is. You want me gone, find my cousin!"

"You know I can't do that. I gather intelligence and convene with the task force. We do not plan rescue missions," Necole told her.

"But I do," Zera said. "That's what I've been doing all these years and I'm not going to stop until I have her back."

Zera walked out of the room then. Her squared shoulders and defiant steps dared the Interpol agent to grab her again or try and stop her in any way. Even though somewhere in the back of her mind, Zera knew that if she actually punched Necole in the face, she would not only end her chances of finding Hiari herself, but she'd also end her chances of ever working in the FBI again. Because Necole would no doubt press charges. And that was a shame because Zera generally liked Necole and everything the woman stood for. She'd told Zera that she was working on the kidnappings across their native country, from the inside. Necole was aware that the money given to fund rescue efforts and to stop the organizations that the combined governments knew were responsible for these horrific acts, was being mishandled. Partially because those in power could do what they wanted and go unchecked and the other part was because nobody cared about the young African girls.

Nobody cared about Hiari, who had planned to become a doctor.

Zera shook her head and took a deep, steadying breath as she approached the door to Ines's room. When she thought she was calm as she could get, Zera entered the room and walked to the bed taking the hand of her friend. The friend Zera had almost gotten killed on her rogue mission.

CHAPTER 12

*T*hree was Dane's limit.

He never drank too much outside the privacy of his home. It wasn't a good look, not that he cared what other people thought of him. Dane cared much more about not losing control in public and possibly hurting himself or someone else.

So when he finished the last of his rum and Coke, Dane pushed the highball glass across the bar and signaled to the bartender for his check. He turned slightly on the stool and looked toward the doorway. He hadn't planned to sit down at the bar at the San Régis for the last forty-five minutes but he wasn't yet ready to go upstairs to that huge suite alone. Not after spending the past five days in the hotel room at the Novotel with Zera.

After years of basically being by himself, Dane did not want to be alone.

Now, he'd settled for the drink to keep him company.

And he'd had way too many, because now he was clearly seeing things.

Suri and a woman had just stood from a table and were now walking toward the door. Dane blinked quickly to clear his vision, but when he looked again Suri definitely had her arm around the woman's waist and the woman had her arm around Suri's shoulder. That wouldn't have normally caught Dane's attention, but when Suri's hand slid down to cup the woman's ass, he'd thought maybe he was hallucinating. That thought was completely squashed as now, the woman turned, taking Suri's face in her hands as she leaned in and kissed her. With tongue.

The kiss ended and the woman left. Suri turned and looked directly at Dane as if she'd known he'd been watching and she'd wanted to put on a show just for him. She gave him a huge smile and began walking toward him.

Dane signaled the bartender and ordered another drink.

"Hey cousin!" Suri said as she climbed onto the stool beside Dane.

"Hi, Suri," he replied.

The moment his drink was delivered Dane took a deep swallow.

"Whoa there," Suri said and reached out to touch his elbow. "Having a rough day?"

"You don't know the half of it," Dane replied.

He was feeling much more relaxed than normal.

"Is this about the FBI lady?" Suri asked and motioned to the bartender to bring her a drink. "I told you the other day it was about a woman."

"Not everything is about a woman," Dane said.

He wondered if that's exactly what he should have been saying to Suri. The reality was he didn't have anything against anyone's career choice or their sexual preference. If Suri was a lesbian, more power to her. If Zera was an FBI agent, more power to her, too. He just really wanted the surprises to stop. For tonight at least.

"But this is about a woman," Suri said. "For you and for me."

Dane had been resting his arms on the bar top, his hands cupping his glass. But at Suri's words, he turned his head to look at her.

"Okay," he said. "I'm assuming everybody knows you're a lesbian since you and your partner weren't really trying to be discreet."

She took a sip of her drink—a mojito—and sat back on the stool before shaking her head.

"I'm not a lesbian," she replied.

Dane was confused.

"I like who I like, when I like them. That's it," she said with a shrug. "That's all I care about. You should try it."

Again, confusion threatened to overtake Dane's liquor and shock-riddled mind.

"I should try what exactly?" he asked.

Suri laughed. "You're cute. You should try only focusing on doing what you like, regardless of any rules or pre-ordained conventions. It's an amazing stress reliever. Even better than sex."

Dane almost groaned. For one, he did not want to think about his younger cousin having sex with the woman he'd just seen, or anyone else for that matter. And he definitely did not want to think about sex with Zera again. Because there would never be sex with Zera again. He picked up his glass.

Suri reached out and put a hand to his wrist stopping him from putting the glass to his lips.

"She kept something big from you. I get it. Lies are tough to deal with. But they can be dealt with if you want to."

Dane sighed. "I don't know what I want."

"I think you do," Suri told him.

"I'm leaving in the morning."

She nodded. "But you're still here tonight."

He shook his head. "I don't know what to say to her. She's not who I thought she was. I don't know who the hell she is."

Suri took his glass. She brought it to her lips and sipped. Then she made a choking sound, her face wrinkled in dissatisfaction as she hurriedly put the glass down on the bar.

"She's the one that has you so twisted up inside that you can't tear yourself away from this nasty as hell drink," Suri said.

Suri picked up her glass and took a longer sip, sighing when she finished as if the mojito was successful in washing away the effects of his drink.

"You only get one life, Dane. And only you can decide how you live it?"

That was the truth. His mother decided how she wanted to live her life and Jaydon decided to follow in her mother's footsteps. They'd both made choices that ultimately ended their lives. In contrast, Dane wanted to make choices that would enrich his life, because he'd been entrenched in way too much death.

"What if I can't deal with who she is, or whatever it is she's doing?"

"What if you go back to the States without even trying to deal with it?"

Dane looked at his cousin whom he'd only known for a short time. She was young and beautiful and smarter than Dane had given her credit for.

"The two of you look good together," he told her. "You look happy."

Suri shrugged. "I am. For now. I try not to get too caught up in the future because I don't know what that will bring. No sense wasting my precious time in the present trying to figure it out."

No, Dane hadn't known Suri Donovan that long, but he liked her. He liked her a lot.

Zera had just stepped out of the shower when she heard the knock at the door. She had no idea how long she'd stood under the spray of hot water but she'd wanted every speck of Ines's blood off her body. Her friend was going to be okay. She was shot in the shoulder and she'd lost a lot of blood, but she was going to make a full recovery.

No thanks to Zera.

She walked to the door, her body still wet, the dress shirt that Dane had left in the closest sticking to her body as she'd hurriedly put it on. She only had a few buttons on the front of the shirt done when the knock became more persistent. It was almost two o'clock in the morning and she had no clue who was on the opposite side of the door. Zera paused and looked for something to use to defend herself. She grabbed the floor lamp that was next to a table a couple feet from the door, yanking the cord from the wall. That probably wasn't smart because it made the room go instantly dark. Still, Zera approached the door. She looked through the peep hole and her breath caught.

Her damp fingers undid the chain and slipped a bit on the doorknob before she could yank it open.

"What are you doing here?" she asked.

Dane stood with his hands on either side of the doorjamb, leaning in slightly. At her question he lifted his head and their gazes locked.

"I want to know what you're doing. And if it's legal, I want to help you get it done so you don't have to be here on your own anymore."

Zera didn't know what to say.

Dane did not look like himself. He'd dropped his arms from the doorjamb to stand in front of her with his legs partially spread, palms flattening first against his jean-clad thighs and then going up to run down the back of his head. His shoulders were slightly slumped and his eyes tinged with red.

"Are you drunk?" she asked.

He sighed heavily and shook his head. Then he shrugged. "I had a couple of drinks, but I'm fine. I didn't drive, I took a taxi. But I needed to see you tonight."

"You're leaving in the morning," she said because she'd been unable to think of hardly anything else since leaving the hospital. "You said you were going back to the States in the morning."

He nodded this time and then took a step back. "Can I please come in?"

Zera stepped out of the way so that he could come inside. She closed and locked the door behind him.

"You won't need this," Dane said and took the lamp out of her hand.

She'd forgotten that she was holding it. Dane was the last person she expected to see tonight. A part of her wanted to be excited that he was here, but another part wasn't sure this was a good sign.

He moved further into the room, going to that window she'd seen him stand at numerous times throughout this past week. Suddenly, Zera felt extremely cool. She looked down to see that she was scarcely dressed and hurriedly buttoned the remaining buttons on the shirt while his back was turned to her. Still feeling a bit off, she sat in one of the chairs across from the couch and waited. Dane apparently had something more to say.

"I should have asked the question that night at the party," he said. "I walked away and didn't ask you what happened. I don't want to do that this time."

Zera crossed her legs. It gave her something to do when she had no idea what to do or to say.

"You came to the hospital and asked questions," she told him.

"Not the right ones," he said and turned to face her. "I should have asked what happened to your cousin and why you felt you had to leave your job to come and look for her on your own?"

She touched the edges of the shirt and licked her lips before speaking. "A friend of mine from home who works for the State Security Agency called me while I was at work one day. He said they had taken Hiari and that my mother and my grandmother were devastated. I knew I had to do something because nobody else would."

"Why do you think nobody else would look for your cousin?"

"Because she's a black girl," Zera immediately replied. "She's a black, Kenyan girl who was just fourteen, coming home from school. She loved going to school and learning new things. She couldn't wait to finish with her studies at home because she planned to go to America for college, just like me."

The last was said quietly as Zera remembered how many times, Hiari had said she wanted to be just like her. They were still fresh in her mind as if Hiari had just leaned over and whispered them in her ear.

"I was in a position to help," she continued. "So I did."

"But you didn't tell your job. Instead you took a leave of absence."

"The kidnapping did not happen on U.S. soil, so it was out of the FBI's jurisdiction. Yes, there are international task forces assigned to such atrocities, but our people never see the help that is reportedly offered. Not in Africa and hardly in the U.S. itself. Besides that, it was my duty. Hiari is my blood. What good was all my education and training if I could not return my cousin to my mother and my grandmother who raised her?"

He looked as if he were trying to understand. Actually, he looked as if he may be pitying her. The thought did not sit well with Zera.

"If you have come out of some sense of obligation, there is no need. I am a big girl, I can handle the end of an affair, Dane."

"The way you handled yourself with Emmet."

Somehow she knew that they were definitely not finished with the subject of Emmet.

"I told you he was part of the job. My friend gave me a name of a person who had been reportedly orchestrating the kidnappings in the regions of Nigeria, Cameroon and Kenya. He was Debare Adebayo. I tracked Debare's movements here to Paris. When I arrived here I learned Debare was just a soldier working for a much bigger organization. Emmet was next up the ladder. And one day when I was doing surveillance on Debare, I ran right into Emmet. I knew that he liked me instantly and I decided to use that."

"But you never slept with him because of his condition?"

"No. I never slept with him," she replied.

"Would you have slept with him if it meant obtaining the information you needed to get your cousin back?" Dane asked.

Again, Zera felt some type of way about Dane's tone and the things that he was saying. She knew he needed answers and a part of her conceded to the fact that she probably owed him some sort of explanation. She did not, however intend to be criticized or judged for her actions. Not by him or anyone else.

Zera dropped her hands from the hem of the shirt and let them rest in her lap. She squared her shoulders as she met Dane's gaze.

"Her name is Hiari Serah Maina. You can say it," she told him. "And when you say her name know that she was more like a little sister to me. Her parents were killed in a senseless confrontation when she was only seven years old. She came to live with my mother and my grandmother when I returned home from school I spent time with Hiari. We both cried when I decided to stay in the U.S. to work, but we talked on the phone almost every day. I wanted the world for her. Every hurdle that I had to jump to get where I was, I wanted out of the way for her to have a smoother path."

Zera stopped. She took a deep breath because those foolish tears were once again threatening to make an appearance.

"So when you ask me if I would have had sex with Emmet if it meant finding Hiari, the answer is yes," she continued. "There is nothing I would not do to bring her and the other girls that were selfishly taken back to their families. Absolutely nothing."

Dane did not speak, but crossed the room to stand in front of her. Zera looked up at him. He knelt down before her slowly and reached out to take her hands.

"I'll help you find Hiari. Whatever resources you need they are at your disposal."

She gasped and one pesky tear slid down her cheek.

Dane reached up, using his finger to brush that tear away. His hand cupped her cheek as he leaned into her. Zera moved too, until her forehead touched his. She closed her eyes and felt extreme relief and comfort, in a way she could never have imagined.

"I just want her back," she whispered after a few quiet moments.

Dane nodded. "We'll get her back," he told her.

Zera opened her eyes then. "Why are you doing this? You can walk away. I won't blame you. I know that this is not your fight."

"It should be all of our fight," Dane said as he pulled back to look at her. "No one person should ever believe they have to do the job of millions. Hiari's and the lives of every girl who has been kidnapped are important. And they should be found, or at the very least every stone that is to be uncovered should be until either they are found or the perpetrators are stopped once and for all."

Damn.

She was in love with him.

Just like that, she knew it and she feared it.

"Thank you," she said and gave him a tentative smile. "Thank you very much for your offer."

Dane shook his head. "Don't turn me down," he said quickly. "And don't turn me away."

His hands found hers again and this time he lifted them to his lips, kissing each of her fingers. "I think I like sleeping in a bed with you, better than I like sleeping alone."

Zera couldn't help it, she chuckled.

"That's funny?"

She continued to laugh even though the look on his face was deadly serious. "A little. Here you are big, bad, sophisticated Dane Donovan and you do not like sleeping alone."

He shrugged. "So my secret's out. Are you going to sell my story to the tabloids now?"

Zera sobered. "Never," she told him. "I would never intentionally do anything to hurt you, Dane."

He kissed her fingers again, and then the inside of her wrists where her pulse quickened. He wrapped her arms around his neck and leaned in to pick her up from the chair. When he was standing and she was in his arms, Dane kissed her lips. Softly at first and then with the signature hunger that always rose fiercely and naturally between them. He carried her to the bedroom where he lay her down on the bed and slowly removed the shirt she'd been wearing.

"My shirt looks good on you," he told her as he stood in the dark room and removed his clothes.

Then he was on the bed with her, pulling her over him as he lay on his back. Zera didn't need any guidance from this point. She reached between them, cupping his already hard shaft in her hands. She angled her hips over him and settled down, loving the feel of the wide crest of his dick pressing eagerly into her center. She rotated her hips, moving down on him slowly, adjusting to the way he so comfortably filled her.

"You feel good inside me," she whispered.

He reached for her and Zera leaned forward so that their lips could meet.

"It feels good to be inside you," he replied and began lifting his hips to pump slowly into her. "Every. Damn. Time."

~

Misha cursed.

He slammed his fist down so hard on the glass table in front of him it cracked, sending spider-like arms over the surface.

"I told you to bring her to me," he said, his voice eerily calm considering the rage that was boiling inside of him. "I gave you one fucking job and you've messed it up twice."

"Third times' the charm," Urod said and chuckled.

It was a sickly sound considering he was still bleeding pretty heavily from the stab wound to his side. Misha had told Luka to bring him here directly from the club and not to offer any type of medical assistance. It served him right for letting one woman take down three of his supposedly best men.

Misha smiled. A cold and sinister smile that Urod mistook for genuine. The idiot continued to laugh as if he was some comedic genius.

The sound died in his throat as Luka came from behind and slid the knife cleanly and effortlessly across his neck.

Misha watched as the body slumped and Luka pushed it to the floor. Urod was an idiot. Not only was his real name— Edouard Dubois—idiotic, but so was his personality. The guy paid absolutely no attention to the plastic that had been laid out on the floor beneath the chair he'd been instructed to sit in upon his arrival at Misha's hotel room. Vigo would be dealt with as well for sending Misha such an inept worker to be promoted.

Segori Belyakov, Misha's father, was getting older. He was also sicker than Segori would ever admit. The *bratva* and all of its branches which stretched from Russia to the United States and everywhere in between, would soon belong to Misha and Vigo. But his younger brother still needed a lot of work before he could rule with the iron hand that Segori had.

"Should we get the vehicles ready to head back?" Luka asked once he'd disposed of Urod's imbecilic body.

Misha stood from his chair. He'd hastily put on a black silk robe when Luka had called him with news of what happened at the club. Now his place was crawling with police.

"You got the girls out safely?" he asked Luka as he walked barefoot over the plush ivory-colored carpet.

"*Da*," Luka replied. "They're in trucks headed to the safe house in London. Armed guards are waiting for their arrival."

"Good," Misha replied.

He was pacing now, going from one end of the lavishly decorated room, to the other, his toes wiggling in the soft carpet.

"We'll close the club for a day or two to let it cool off. It will be a loss, but we will make it up with a new shipment coming in next week," Luka promised.

Misha was confident they would make up the loss. Even if they had to change the payment agreements with some of their more high-profiled clients to do so. He continued to pace.

"Where is she now?" he asked finally.

"She left the hospital and went to a hotel," Luka replied. "Abram and Evgeni are right outside the hotel waiting for your orders. But there's someone else there watching her too. Probably police."

Misha nodded.

"Probably," Misha said. "We will have to be careful. I want

her, but I do not want the attention. Tell them to stay with her for now. I have to make a call."

Luka left Misha alone and Misha pulled his phone from the pocket of the robe. He made a call that would decide which one of the Belyakov brothers would rule the *bratva* and which one would be buried beside their father.

CHAPTER 13

"So you took my advice?" Suri asked Dane at breakfast the next afternoon.

They were sitting at the table in the designated dining area of the suite at the San Régis.

"All things considered, it did make sense to bring Zera here last night," Dane replied.

Today Suri wore a red high-waist skirt, white blouse with puffy sleeves and bright yellow sandals with ties that went all the way up to her knee. She wore yellow make-up at her eyes and fire engine-red on her lips. Her hair was twisted in some fashion that left it piled high on top of her head.

"Of course it made sense," Suri insisted after finishing her second plum.

A bowl of fruit sat in the center of the table, a carafe with coffee and a pitcher of water on either side of it. Dane enjoyed fruits over vegetables and agreed with Suri's obvious appreciation of the small summer plum. They were called

Mirabelles and Dane was certain he'd never had one in the States.

He finished the water he'd been drinking and set the glass on the table.

"That's why I suggested you do it," Suri continued. "I knew once you went to see her that things would work out. And they did."

Dane had to agree with her and was more than a little amused at how happy that seemed to make her.

Suri wiped her hands on a linen napkin and sat back in the chair. "When I got your text, however I wanted to both strangle and kiss you. I do not need a babysitter, but thank you for being concerned."

Dane gave her a brief smile.

"I did not say you needed a babysitter, Suri. I simply wanted to make sure you were safe."

She arched a brow. "You wanted to make sure I wasn't necking with another woman in the bar at four in the morning," Suri said. "You didn't fool me for a second."

His smile turned into a chuckle.

Dane called Suri last night, or rather very early this morning. After his conversation with Zera and their subsequent joining, Dane had lay in bed staring at the ceiling. Zera had once again wrapped her body around his, her breath whispered warmly over his chest while thoughts continued to run through his mind. He was worried about Zera's safety and how best to protect her. He was also concerned about how everything that Zera was going through could ultimately impact his businesses and the new Donovan Oilwell endeavor.

That train of thought had led him back to his newfound family and how unexpectedly helpful Suri had been. He eased out of the bed, removed his cell phone from the charger and left the room. Dane sent a text to Suri, thanking her for her sage advice and telling her that he hoped she was safe and sound in bed. He had been shocked when she'd immediately responded asking if he'd taken her advice why was he on his cell phone instead of making sweet love to his woman. Suri made Dane laugh, something he hadn't done enough of in his life. They'd exchanged text messages for almost fifteen minutes, during which time Dane admitted to being worried about Zera's safety.

"That's not what I was thinking, but since you brought it up, I'm glad you were safe and in your suite by that time," he told her. "It was a good idea to get Zera out of the Novotel. It hadn't occurred to me that if someone were after her they may have followed her back there."

"That's because your mind was sex-addled at the time," Suri said. "But seriously, her safety should be considered. As soon as Roark told me and Ridge about who she was and what she was to you, I thought about the danger. Of course, Roark with his business-first-last-and-only mentality, thought about the companies. And Ridge's thoughts went to the family."

"But you think with your heart," Dane said.

He admired that about his cousin.

Suri shrugged. "I like to think that makes me smarter than everyone else."

It just might, Dane thought.

"I appreciate you sending your driver to pick us up," he told her. "He did exactly as instructed, coming around to the back service entrance. I had to speak to the concierge and hotel's general manager about us going down the service elevator and through the kitchen to leave. But it all worked out."

"How is your FBI agent this morning?" Suri asked him.

She had been calling Zera since last night. At first Dane had remained caught up on the "FBI agent" part. Now, he thought more about the fact that Suri believed that Zera belonged to him.

"She was exhausted," he said. "After everything that happened at that club, her friend's surgery and me confronting her, she was completely drained. I was able to convince her to have breakfast in bed this morning."

Suri grinned with a knowing look in her eyes. "I'll just bet she was exhausted by all of that and by all that great make up sex you two had!"

Dane shook his head. "You're incorrigible."

Suri tossed her head back and laughed. "I concur," she said between guffaws.

"You told LeAmbette I was still here," Zera said to Aasir when he'd finally returned her messages, later that afternoon.

When she'd asked Dane this morning how he'd found out she was FBI, he'd told her that his cousin was a profiler and he'd come across her name and pictures of her and Dane together in one of his cases, Zera knew that her cover was blown. Maybe not with the Belyakov *bratva*, but she was definitely no longer working under the government radar.

"I needed someone to keep an eye on you," he replied. "I told you it was time for you to come home. You almost got yourself killed."

"No," Zera said sadly. "I almost got my friend killed."

She'd called the hospital once this morning and then again after she and Dane had finished with lunch. That was how she came to be in the bedroom of this beautiful suite at the San Régis, while Dane was in the outer rooms. He had business to take care of and she'd wanted some privacy to make her own calls.

After hearing from the nurse that Ines was stable, Zera immediately dialed Aasir's personal cell number.

"I'm sorry she was hurt, but I am relieved that you weren't," Aasir said. "Enough is enough, Zera. This is over. I should never have given you all the information I did. Not only could I ultimately lose my job for my involvement in your search, but you could have died."

"But I didn't," Zera told him.

She'd thought about that all last night. She was alive and Ines was alive. But what about Hiari? And what about the girls?

"Those leads in that agenda book are big, Aasir. They could bring down multiple kidnapping rings and save so many lives. How can I stop now?"

"Give Necole the book. She'll add it to the information the task force has compiled and they'll handle this. They are much better equipped to handle it than you can on your own."

Zera listened to his words. They were similar to some of the thoughts she'd had last night while she'd sat in Ines's room holding her hand.

It had been four years and while Zera had made some progress, she hadn't been successful in figuring out exactly where Hiari had been taken. She'd hoped that eventually she would gather enough information on Emmet to get him to tell her everything. But then Emmet had been killed. The explosion at the office building where Emmet operated a legitimate accounting firm and his illegal money laundering and human trafficking empire had come just a week after Emmet's last trip to the French Riviera. It was after that trip that Emmet had placed the money and the agenda book in his safe. Zera wondered now if Emmet had known that Misha Belyakov was going to order his death.

"I know where they took her," she told Aasir. "I've worked so long and so hard for this. I want to find her."

"Then let Necole do her job. Give her the information and come home, Zera. Come back to Nairobi. Your mother and grandmother miss you terribly."

Zera sighed. "I spoke to them yesterday morning."

She realized now that she'd called them because she knew she was planning to go after Pierre and Luka yesterday and some part of her must have known how dangerous that was.

"It's over, Zera."

She shook her head. "Not for me, Aasir. And I apologize for putting your job at jeopardy. I appreciate all the information you've been able to pass onto me. If I'm ever asked, I promise not to divulge my sources."

"Necole already knows I was helping you," he said. "Luckily her family is very close to mine so we've always been more like relatives than colleagues even though she prefers to make London her home with her husband. We all want to bring our girls home, Zera. We do. We're just trying to do so while working in the guidelines that have been set for us."

And that was the problem, Zera thought. The guidelines were too damn restraining.

"I appreciate all of your help, I really do. I'm safe and after last night I think my investigation will get a push in the right direction."

"After you walked into the arms of the *bratva* and barely escaped? Are you kidding?"

"No," she told him. "I am not talking about that. I mean, those events obviously set things in motion, but I won't be working alone anymore. A fr...uh, I mean, someone I've known, or rather...," she paused and sighed. "I'm going to have some help now. So this might actually be over soon. But not yet, Aasir. Not until—"

"Not until you know for sure whether Hiari is dead or alive. I get it, Zera. Who is this friend that is going to help you? And do you think it's wise to get some outsider involved?" he asked.

"His name is Dane. He's a wealthy American and he has resources that I can use to open more doors. I can follow the trail that was outlined in Emmet's book and hopefully figure out a way to fill in the blanks where he left out Hiari and her group's final destination," she told him.

"Why is he helping you? What does he want in return?"

"Nothing," Zera replied. "And why do you say it like that?"

She felt like he was accusing her of something, but not actually having the guts to come right out and say what.

"I'll say it one more time, let Necole and the rest of us do our jobs, Zera."

"It is my job!" she told him. "She is my family. My grandmother wants me to bring her home and I promised her I would."

For Zera, that was all that mattered. She ended the call with Aasir after he agreed to visit her family to let them know that she was doing well, but still disagreed with her working with Dane.

Zera refused to focus on Aasir or his pessimism right now. She walked out of the room and entered the sitting area that was now full of people. One of which was familiar.

"Zera," Dane said and immediately walked toward her.

He touched her elbow and walked beside her until they were standing in the center of the room.

"These are my cousins, Roark and Suri Donovan and Agent Cade Donovan. Cade is with the FBI. And this is—"

"Agent Necole LeAmbette," Zera finished for him. "Nice to see you again."

Zera gave the Interpol agent a bleak smile, but she looked to Dane's cousins and gave them a more genuine one.

Roark stood with his arms folded across his chest. He wore black slacks and a white Polo shirt. His complexion, a soft buttery hue, was lighter than Dane's. But Roark's black hair, thick brows and light beard gave him a darker, more brooding look. Cade also had a lighter complexion than Dane's. He wore a black suit, crisp white shirt and a black tie which gave him a definite federal agent appearance. The gold watch at one wrist and thick link bracelet on the other said he was not as straight an arrow as his job might entail.

"Hi, Zera. It's a pleasure to finally meet you," the woman named Suri said.

She also extended her hand for Zera to shake. Zera happily did so.

"It's a pleasure to meet you, Suri."

The woman's smile was as bright as her yellow eye shadow and sandals. Her hair was beautifully and boldly styled and Zera thought she could definitely like her.

"We need to talk, Zera," Cade said and motioned for Zera to take a seat.

Dane, once again touching her elbow, steered her to the couch and waited until she sat. He sat beside her.

Necole and Suri took seats in the chairs across from the couch, while Roark and Cade remained standing.

"I understand that my name came up in a case you're working on, Agent Donovan. But I'm not totally sure why," Zera said.

"Call me, Cade," he said with a quick smile. "After hearing about last night's events, I decided I needed to make a visit to Paris. Luckily, the Donovans have two private jets."

"Three," Suri chimed in. "Dane's got one too."

Suri smiled, but Dane kept the somber look on his face after that little announcement.

Cade continued. "I'm speaking totally off the record today. The Bureau has an international team that works directly with Interpol on a variety of cases, so I'm a little out of jurisdiction on this one."

"Join the club," Necole stated. "This is also an unofficial meeting on behalf of my office and the international task force I am attached to."

Okay, all disclaimers had been made, Zera thought. That meant this little meeting was not going to be good.

"This all sounds very official," Suri said. "I might need a drink. Can I get anyone something?"

The men each gave Suri a slight shake of their head, while Necole smiled with her "no thanks". Zera, on the other hand, quite agreed with Suri.

"Yes. Please. A glass of wine would be great," she said.

"There have been a half dozen murders in the States stretching from New Mexico to Rhode Island. Each victim with ties, both current and past, to Russian organizations that were already on an international watch list," Cade said. "My team was asked to review the case files and to provide a profile on the killer. In doing so, I came across your name."

"In what capacity?" Zera asked.

She accepted the glass from Suri and took a tentative sip. Her goal was to appear calm, when she was actually feeling a little ill. Zera had no idea what Cade was going to say next, but she knew it could only get worse.

Cade unbuttoned his suit jacket and slipped a hand into his front pant pocket. He looked like a GQ cover. While, off to the side, Roark put her more in mind of Heathcliff, the brooding hero in *Wuthering Heights*, one of Zera's favorite books.

"You once provided a report on a man named Thaddeus Trudeau in reference to a series of phone calls, meetings and email transmission intercepted via a FISA warrant. Your report emphasized that the Bureau had no evidence to connect Trudeau to any of the cybercrimes that were being investigated. So no arrest was made."

Zera remembered the report clearly because it was one of the first she'd worked on at the Bureau. The warrant obtained through the Foreign Intelligence Surveillance Court was specific on the messages that could be used in their investigation so it had been a colossal headache sorting through all of the intelligence, making sure to only focus on what they could use legally.

"I remember that," was all Zera said in response.

Cade nodded. "Trudeau is the latest murder victim. His body was found six weeks ago. Information concerning a disagreement between Trudeau and the organization he worked for made an easy murder plot. But not a professional hit. So investigators had to dig deeper. Your report was in Trudeau's file, but when the investigating agent tried to reach you to discuss, he discovered you'd taken a leave of absence. A four-year leave of absence and that you'd left the States. You hadn't returned to Nairobi and the last trace of you traveling had been to Paris. A city where Misha Belyakov runs a very lucrative leg of the Belyakov *bratva*, the organized crime family that Trudeau was connected to."

Zera could easily follow Cade's train of thought from there. Her report had kept Trudeau out of federal custody, allowing him to go on for the next four years and commit whatever other crimes he had committed in that time. Those crimes quite possibly led to Trudeau's death. Years later there's trouble brewing between Trudeau and the Russian mafia. And the agent who let him go free is on leave. Had she been working for the Belyakovs too? And, if so, after she did her job of keeping Trudeau out of jail, had she then traveled to Paris to perform another job for the organization? It made sense on a basic level, even if it was totally untrue.

"I'm not working with the Belyakovs," she stated evenly.

"We know that now," Cade said.

"After I spoke with you last night, Zera, I felt it was time to clear some of the air," Necole added.

Zera looked at her. "What exactly do you mean by that?"

"As I told you last night I believe you've done all you can here with regard to your cousin's case. The Belyakovs want to get their hands on you so badly that they were willing to shoot up their own club, bringing the eyes of the police right to their door. You know something, or you have something they want and they aren't going to stop until they kill you to get it." Necole spoke in an eerily calm voice, but her words had Dane reaching for Zera's hand.

And Zera's heart beat wildly.

"So since we're now certain that you're not working against us," Cade interjected. "We need to protect you."

"We need to know everything you learned from Emmet Parks," Necole said.

Zera's hand began to shake, so she hurriedly finished her wine. She toyed with the stem of the glass for a few seconds, feeling the eyes of everyone in that room on her.

"I knew Emmet Parks," Dane said. "We went to college together. Are you certain that he had enough information to hurt a Russian crime family in some way?"

Necole shrugged and kept her gaze focused on Zera. "Only she can tell us that."

"And what happens when she tells you?" Dane asked.

"We take over the investigation and she gets out of sight," Cade answered.

Dane continued. "And what about Hiari? Does your investigation involve finding her and the other girls that were kidnapped?"

Silence ensued and Zera sighed.

She slipped her hand away from Dane's and stood. Walking to the bar across the room, she set the glass on the bar top and stood with her back to everyone for a few seconds. She took deep steadying breaths and thought about her next words carefully before turning back to face them.

Dane was staring at her with concern, a look she hadn't seen on him before, but one that touched her heart with warm fingers that seemed to tighten their grip with each second that passed. Roark had relaxed his stance only slightly, but still looked at her with leery eyes. Suri and Necole sat quietly. Cade was waiting. He had already profiled her so it was a good possibility he knew exactly what she was getting ready to say.

"The reason I left the FBI to come here alone and look for Hiari is because I knew that nobody else was going to do it. The years have passed and there have been more times than I can recall that I felt like I was wasting my time. Like I was never going to find her. But then there would be a clue. I'd overhear Emmet on the phone with an associate mentioning kidnappings in South Africa. Or I'd find notes in Emmet's pockets with numbers about groups that were being taking out of the country and brought to the UK or other places to be put up for sale. Each time I thought it was time to stop, I received more signs that I needed to continue and so I did. Now you want me to walk away and let you handle it. But you haven't given me any assurances that you *will* actually handle this situation," Zera told them.

"We do not operate in assurances, Zera. You already know that," Necole said.

"Then I don't tell you a damn thing," was Zera's retort. "If you cannot assure me that real efforts will be taken to follow the leads I've uncovered on my own, then I will keep them to myself and find my cousin on my own."

She'd said on her own but Zera had immediately looked to Dane. To her surprise and utter joy, he nodded his agreement with what she'd said.

"Then you have it," Cade spoke up before Necole could. "Necole leads the case through Interpol, I'll stay connected only through the Trudeau link. But that will just be how we document it on paper. You give us this information, Zera, and I guarantee you that I will do everything in my power to find out what happened to your cousin."

"So she tells you what she knows and then she gets gone," Suri said. "That makes sense. And I know the perfect place she can go. To the Donovan country house in Le Boulay. It's lovely there this time of year and my mother and Aunt Birdie are already there planning a family gathering to take place in a couple of days. It's secluded and she'll still remain close enough that if you need her for more information you can get to her more easily than if she returns to the U.S."

All eyes had turned to Suri while she spoke. Then, as if waiting with baited breath, they all shifted to Zera.

She looked at Dane. Their gazes held while thoughts soared through her mind. Dane had assured her he would help and Zera was both touched and eager to get started. But maybe Aasir had been right in keeping Necole in the loop. The task force assigned to working on these cases would be the ideal place for this investigation to continue. And with Cade's connections, things could get moving even faster than if they only worked with Dane's resources. Because Dane wasn't in the FBI.

"I've resigned myself to the fact that I've probably already lost my job. And I will eventually get over my part in getting Ines shot. But what I absolutely cannot do is ever return to my home in Kenya if I do not find out what happened to Hiari." Her voice cracked as she said her cousin's name.

Dane stood and walked to her. He took her hand and brought it up to his lips to kiss.

"I promised you we would find out and that offer still stands. Whichever route you decide to take I'll help you. But I do have to say that your safety is a priority. It has to be considered," he told her.

Zera agreed. Getting herself killed would not help Hiari or any of the other girls.

"Your family has a country house in Le Boulay. I never thought about meeting your family," she said.

"Neither did I," he replied.

"They're going to love both of you!" Suri exclaimed.

CHAPTER 14

*L*e *Boulay, Centre, France*

Two days later, three black SUVs with bulletproof tinted glass windows and two Interpol agents in each drove away from the San Régis hotel. Each SUV went in different directions at the first intersection. A silver sedan trailed them. Police officers were in the sedans. Dane and Zera were in one of the SUVs. They'd once again used the back exit of the hotel leaving in the middle of the night. Security was a big issue when threats by the mafia were a real thing. That was exactly what Zera had to explain to Ines and her grandmother at the hospital yesterday.

"The police have arrested Pierre. He'll be charged with manufacturing and distributing drugs," Zera said as she'd stood next to Ines's bed.

Frances Buling was seated in a cushioned chair on the other side of the bed, her weathered skin sagging a bit at the jaw, her piercing blue eyes intent on Zera.

Ines's right arm was in a sling so that she wouldn't move it too much and irritate her shoulder wound. Her hair looked darker against the white pillowcase as it spread out around her face. The color in her cheeks was coming back. The night of the shooting she'd been so pale and unresponsive. Zera had been scared to death of losing her.

"I can't believe he was working with a real live mafia," Ines said.

"I'm so sorry I involved you," Zera told her. "I should have taken you home instead of letting you go to the club with me."

"I wanted to go," Ines said. "If I recall correctly, I insisted."

"But you shouldn't have. I shouldn't have," Zera told her. "Now, you'll have to move."

"Are you kidding? I've been dying to move to the U.S.," Ines said.

"I have not," was her grandmother's retort.

Zera felt like scum.

"I am truly sorry, Ms. Buling. I did not intend for any of this to happen, but the police want to make sure that you and Ines are totally safe from any possible retaliation attempts," Zera said.

So, thanks to Cade pulling some strings with a friend of his at the U.S. Marshals Service, Ines and her grandmother would be temporarily treated as if they were part of the United States Federal Witness Protection Program. Zera hated that this would halt Ines's career for the time being and she hated that now Ines was going to have a scar on her gorgeous body. This entire situation sucked and made Zera even more eager to get Luka and the Belyakovs.

"She'll be fine," Ines said. "And once this is all over I'm going to New York to find an agent. I know you're thinking that I will not be able to model, but I will. Just as you will find your cousin. Because bad things happen, Zera. We do not have power to stop them. We just have the power to go on."

Now, as Zera sat in the backseat of the SUV, Ines's words echoed in her head. *Bad things happen.* Zera could relate to that and still be pissed off at the fact that bad things just kept happening around her.

Dane reached out to take her hand. At first the touch startled her, but it didn't take long for warmth and comfort to sink in. He had been holding her hand a lot in the past few days, and sticking much closer to her than Zera thought he ever would. She knew the reason why and had to wonder what would happen when this was all over.

Even in the dark of night Zera could clearly see that Suri had made an understatement. The SUV came to a slow stop and waited while black iron gates opened slowly in front of them. The SUV moved forward and Zera's breath caught. Perfectly manicured bushes more than six feet tall lined the cobblestone pathway to the house, or rather the chateau, before them. It was huge and stately. Zera couldn't wait to see it in the light of day. Minutes later the SUV came to a stop. The agent sitting on the second row in front of them, turned back to say, "I will check a few things out first. I'll come back to get you."

He got out leaving the second agent and the driver in the front seats, with Dane and Zera on the third row.

"I don't like this," she whispered to Dane.

"You don't like being chauffeured and staying in lavish French chateaus?" he asked.

She looked over to him, the dark interior of the car casting his face in shadows. The joking tone in his voice was clear, but his outside appearance was just as serious as ever.

"I would have preferred doing both those things without

armed guards," she replied. "Because then I could have rode you during the drive to the chateau."

The temperature in the SUV increased instantly and Dane's fingers tightened around hers.

"Don't tempt me," he said.

"We're not alone," she reminded him.

"We will be," he replied.

Before Zera could comment, there was a knock on the window. The agent in the front seat got out. There was a momentary pause before he stuck his head back into the SUV and gave them the okay to come out.

They stepped out and were escorted up the stairs and to the double doors. It was opened immediately and a man dressed in black pants, white shirt and white jacket answered. His hair was snowy white, his skin an olive tone and his eyes a warm brown.

"Good evening, Mr. Donovan. I am Carlisle. Your room is ready," he said, his French accent heavy and romantic.

Zera thought he looked like he could have been James Bond in a previous movie.

The foyer was breathtaking. The French Victorian décor not overwhelming, but complimenting the space. Heavy drapes hung at the large windows along the wall going up the stairs. Light-colored hardwood floors with the planks laid in an intricate circular pattern glistened while the mural painted on the walls throughout the foyer boasted a lovely country theme that Zera was certain would resonate throughout the entire house.

"We'll stay until morning and then a new shift will arrive," the agent told them. "You'll have a team of four with you while you're here until Agent LeAmbette advises us of a new plan.

Nyle, the driver, will stay on once we leave. If you go anywhere, Nyle will take you."

"Thank you," Dane said and shook both the agents' hand.

Zera did the same and watched as Carlisle directed the men to a door at the end of the foyer.

Carlisle led Dane and Zera up the stairs and down a long hall where a gorgeous beige and dark green rug lined the floor. Their room was at the end. Carlisle opened the door and stood aside while they walked in.

"I will bring your bags to you momentarily," he stated.

"Thank you, Carlisle," Dane said.

Zera found a light switch on the wall near the door. She gasped once the room was illuminated.

"I feel like royalty," she said as she looked around.

Floor to ceiling windows, elegant drapes in a butter yellow and rich blue color. A plush blue rug covered most of the floor, matching blue arm chairs with an ivory colored table filled the center of the room. While a huge bed with a matching blue footboard dominated the space. A crystal chandelier hung from the ceiling while a small table and two chairs sat close to a set of French doors.

"It is a stunning room," Dane said.

She turned to him. "Stunning good or stunning bad?"

He came to her, lacing his arms around her waist and pulling her close. "As in I cannot wait to get you into that stunning bed."

Zera's heart pounded and her center throbbed.

Suddenly, being sent to a country chateau for protection didn't seem like such a bad idea.

∼

Bridgette "Birdie" Donovan sat in a chair at the end of a twelve-foot long dining room table. Sunlight poured into the windows around her, casting the woman in an ethereal glow. She wore a light pink pantsuit with a cream-colored blouse, a single strand of iridescent pink pearls at her neck and pearl studs in her ears. There was a gaudy tiered diamond ring on her right ring finger and her hair was cut ruthlessly straight stopping just before her shoulders. But none of that seemed as striking to Dane as the color of Aunt Birdie's hair. It started black at the roots, then gradually turned a lighter gray color, before the frosty white edges left him speechless. Dane was sure he'd never seen anything like it before.

Birdie was the only girl and youngest child of Rowan and Adeline Donovan. She was ninety years old, had no children and had never married. She'd also never worked a day in her life. Thanks to her inheritance from her parents and the increasing worth of her shares in Donovan Oilwell, she never had to. She owned a house in her hometown of Beaumont, Texas but spent most of her time traveling or harassing the staff at the Donovan family-owned Camelot Resort on Sansonique, their private Caribbean island. In a family as big as the Donovans, Birdie had chosen to spend the majority of her days alone. Dane would soon learn the reason why a solitary life suited the silver-tongued heiress.

"So you're Bernard's son," she said in an accusatory tone.

Dane was the only one in the room with her at the moment as Aunt Maxine had hurriedly whisked Zera off the second they stepped out of the bedroom this morning. If Dane didn't know better he would swear the woman had been waiting for them. This was his first time meeting Maxine Donovan as well, but there was no time for real introductions.

The short woman with the warm smile had greeted them and then offered to show Zera the gardens, right after she'd told Dane that Aunt Birdie was waiting for him in the formal dining room.

"Yes ma'am," Dane answered his aunt.

Birdie continued as if he hadn't responded. "And your mama was the one running around killing folk and causing all kinds of mayhem."

Aunt Birdie had stopped looking at him. She was now using a shiny silver knife to butter the smallest piece of croissant Dane had ever seen a person try to eat.

She was his complexion, her skin a little leathery, and her lips were painted a pinkish-brown hue.

Dane had taken a seat in a chair to Aunt Birdie's right.

"I guess people don't much listen to the words in the Holy Bible anymore," she said. "Thou shalt not kill is self-explanatory."

She opened her mouth and set the piece of croissant on her tongue as if it were a delicacy and began chewing slowly. Dane wasn't sure what he was supposed to say to her offensive diatribe, so he opted to pour himself a cup of coffee instead.

"And you had a sister too, I heard. But she wasn't Bernard's child. He has two daughters by two other women. I always knew that boy was gonna cause trouble. I used to tell my brother, Ike, he needed to get those boys of his in line. Both Ike and Dot spoiled all six of those boys terribly. And now we have you." She said the last with a tilt of her head in his direction.

She acted as if she were having a conversation with herself and Dane was just there as some sort of prop. He didn't really appreciate that.

"It's nice to meet you, Aunt Birdie. I understand you've just returned from a Mediterranean cruise," Dane said after putting sugar in his coffee.

"A cruise can be delightful without all those rude folk to go with it. They just let anybody on a ship these days. And don't interrupt me, chile. Just like your daddy, I swear."

She shook her head and Dane drank from his cup. This was going to be a long morning.

"Got yourself in some trouble with a woman. If you Donovan men could just keep it in your pants, things would be a lot simpler around here."

Aunt Birdie continued to talk and Dane continued to interject with his own comments. It was clear to him that his dear opinionated aunt loved to hear herself talk. As Dane currently had a lot of things on his mind, he was content to let her do just that.

Later that evening, Aunt Birdie had a larger audience to spend her time insulting.

There had been a flurry of activity going on throughout the seven bedroom, and five bathroom house. Caterers and florists moved about while family members arrived. Apparently, this summer gathering was a big deal. Luckily for Dane and Zera, it was a casual big deal because neither of them had anything more formal than a sundress or a business suit to wear.

"Maxine seems really nice," Zera said.

From the chair where he sat, Dane had been able to watch her standing in the mirror doing all the things that women do to get dressed. Tonight, she wore a long white dress in a big blue flower print. A thin gold belt wrapped around her waist and high-heeled natural-colored sandals were clasped at her ankles.

If he'd seen the dress hanging in a store, he might have called it boring and dismissed it totally. But on Zera's tall and slightly curvy frame, the wispy material seemed fluid and engaging. The fact that he hadn't been able to take his eyes off her basically proved that point.

To be fair, Dane had also been mesmerized by the way her fingers moved masterfully to style her hair. She'd pulled it into a twisty bun angled more on the back right side of her head. She fastened big hoop earrings to her ears and pushed a half dozen gold bangles onto her arm. The make-up she wore was applied quickly. It was a lot less than Suri wore, but enhanced Zera's beauty just as much.

"Do you think the rest of them will like me?" she asked.

"The rest of who?" Dane asked.

She sighed as she turned to face him, one hand on her hip. "You weren't listening to me were you? I guess it's starting to happen already you not paying attention to me because we've been together all day every day for the past few days."

"I don't think I could ever get tired of being with you," Dane said.

The words shocked him probably as much as the widening of her eyes said they surprised her.

Zera cleared her throat as if she'd been the one to say something. "I asked if you thought the rest of your family was going to like me?"

"Come here," he said.

For a second she looked as if she weren't going to move, but then she walked toward him. A sexier sight Dane did not think he'd ever seen before. No parts of her body were bared to him but her arms and yet a punch of desire slammed into his gut and was now blossoming throughout his body.

"Turn around," he told her when she was only a few steps away.

She gave him a questioning gaze, but once again obliged.

As she turned, the bottom half of the dress lifted slightly in the air, whirling around her like the skirt on a ballroom dancer. Dane stood quickly in the middle of her last turn, catching her at the waist. She came to a stop facing him, her hands going to his shoulders.

"I like you," he told her sincerely. "I like you wearing this flowery dress. And I like you in your polka dot tennis shoes. I even like how you managed to swim more laps than me this afternoon."

Her smile was slow but it lifted her cheekbones and lightened her brown eyes, making his heart do an odd type of flutter in his chest.

"But I asked if you thought your family was going to like me," she said, her voice softer.

Dane shook his head. "Doesn't matter. None of this matters, Zera."

She blinked but didn't seem able to speak. Dane sort of liked that too. He was taking her by surprise, tossing things at her that she couldn't explain or rebut. It was new for both of them, but Dane liked it. And, he realized with a start, he had more he wanted to say to her.

"Come on you two. You can't hide from Aunt Birdie forever," Suri said after knocking loudly on the door of their room.

Zera laughed. "I've managed to avoid meeting the infamous Aunt Birdie, but I've heard more than enough about her."

Dane stepped back away from her, taking her hand as he

walked toward the door. "Nothing you've heard can prepare you for Bridgette Donovan."

They left the room and walked down the stairs, but it wasn't until they entered the living room where everyone was gathered that the show actually began.

"Look who just arrived," Maxine said after she stepped back from hugging two adorable twin girls.

"Linc Donovan and his wife Jade," Dane told Zera as they moved closer to where everyone was hugging Linc and Jade. "Their daughters are Torian and Tamala. They're ten years old."

"They're beautiful," Zera said.

Dane looked over to see her staring at the two girls who were standing next to their mother.

"Dane. It's good to see you here," Linc said when Dane and Zera had finally stood in front of them.

Dane shook his cousin's hand and leaned in for a one-arm hug. Linc and Dane were close in height and had close to the same complexion. They were also very close in age. Only three months made Dane older, but those three months had been enough to shake up the entire Donovan family with the arrival of a newcomer.

"Hi, Dane!" Jade said excitedly as she stepped up to hug him.

Dane hugged her back. "Hello, Jade," he said and held back the confession that it was also good to see her.

"It seems like forever since you've been out to the West Coast," Jade said. "I told you when you come back, you have to visit the spa for a massage."

While Linc Donovan owned two casinos, The Gramercy I in

Las Vegas and The Gramercy II in St. Michael's, Maryland, Jade owned and operated full-service spa called Happy Hands.

"I know. I was planning a trip out there once I returned." He paused and then cleared his throat before saying, "Uncle Henry and Uncle Everette want to learn more about the new company we're forming here so I told them I'd come out to brief them on it."

"That's good," Linc said. "It's very good. You're bringing us into the next generation."

"I'd say you're doing just fine bringing in the next generation yourself," Dane told Linc with a nod to the girls.

He'd been so busy talking to Linc and Jade and trying to understand the whirlwind of emotions going through him—first when he'd been upstairs with Zera and now, at seeing Linc and Jade again—that he hadn't noticed Zera had been in a conversation with the girls.

"Oh hello," Zera said when she realized all eyes were now on her. "I'm Zera Kennedy."

"She's really from Africa, Daddy," Torian said.

The twins had Jade's hazel eyes, and their curly dark brown hair was pulled up into bushy-ended ponytails.

"Yeah, listen to her talk," Tamala added. "Say something again!"

Zera smiled but Dane watched as Jade cringed and Linc looked shocked.

"I am so sorry," Jade hurried to tell Zera. "They meant no offense. Did you girls?"

The girls were both shaking their heads.

"Of course they didn't," Linc added. "Hello, I'm Lincoln Donovan and you've already met my daughters, Torian and Tamala."

Zera nodded and accepted Linc's outstretched hand to shake. "Yes. You have beautiful children, Lincoln" she said and the girls giggled.

"She's lovely, Dane. What took you so long introducing us," Jade said pushing past Dane and Linc until she could stand near Zera. "I'm Jade. It's nice to meet you, Zera."

And with that Jade and the twins whisked Zera off to the other side of the room. Aunt Birdie was on the other side of the room, sitting on a couch near the Baby Grand piano. Dane immediately heard his aunt proclaim, "Oh she's finally here. For a minute I thought the spy was just going to continue to spy on us and not socialize at all."

He sighed and Linc clapped him on the shoulder with one hand.

"Gotta love Aunt Birdie," he said with a chuckle.

Dane couldn't help but frown. "Is she like this all the time?"

"Most of the time," Linc said. "The good thing is once she gives you the third-degree you're in the family and she actually starts to care about what you do with yourself. Aunt Birdie is one hundred percent old school, especially about marriage and having babies. So a piece of advice—if you're as in love with Zera as the way you're staring at her seems to suggest, then marry her quickly and start having babies soon. That'll make Aunt Birdie happy."

"We're not there yet," Dane replied quickly. "I mean, we haven't even talked about any kind of future. This is just temp..." Dane stopped before he could say what he was doing with Zera was temporary. The word and that theory seemed wrong.

"Yeah. Okay, I've definitely been where you are so I won't push. Just sayin' that's how Aunt Birdie works," Linc told him.

"Thanks for the advice," Dane said.

A few minutes later they all moved to the dining room. Maxine, Roark, Ridge and Suri sat on one side of the table, while Dane, Zera, Jade, Linc and the twins sat on the other side. Aunt Birdie sat at the head of the table, tossing out orders to the staff and looking around the table, making statements to each of her family members.

"Mama and Daddy would have been proud," Aunt Birdie said when they were all finishing their dessert.

Dane had been watching Zera as she talked animatedly with the girls. They'd been chatting all throughout dinner and Zera didn't seem the least bit bothered by it.

"They loved their big family. Granpop Elias and Gran—her name was Gertrude, but we called her Gran, they used to have reunions at The D Ranch down in Gillespie, Texas. My brothers would bring their wives and children. Uncle Charleston would bring his wife, and children and they would bring their spouses and children, and we just had a good time with a big 'ole BBQ and swimming in the lake. The lake here is pretty, but there's really no place like home."

Everyone grew silent as they looked down at Aunt Birdie and listened to what she was saying.

"That's what it's all about. The love and the loyalty that family has. Now you, gal," she said and looked straight at Zera. "You got some things going on, but you know about family. I heard it in your voice when I asked you to tell me about your mother and grandmother. And you know about loyalty too, or you wouldn't be here doing what you're doing." She waved a hand at the shocked looks at the table. "Look, I know what's going on around here, even if y'all don't tell me. And I'm here to say that things are gonna work out just like they're supposed to. Y'all remember that. Whether it's good or bad, it's how it's supposed to be. And nobody can change what's supposed to be. You just gotta keep going."

There was something in what she'd said, something solid and true that touched a part of Dane. What was happening to him? All day long he'd felt one overwhelming emotion after another. Now, all those emotions seemed to be coming together in a way that he had to figure out how to deal with.

"And you see those twins down there, looking so much alike I can't hardly remember which one is which?"

When nobody answered, Aunt Birdie reached over and tapped Zera on the arm.

"Those two you've been talking to," Aunt Birdie continued. "I know you like 'em and that's good, because I want you to know I don't plan on dying until I see the babies you and Bernard's son will create. I got a feeling they'll be just as ornery as Bernard was when he was young."

Zera looked at Dane, shock and embarrassment clear on her face. And Dane looked from her to Linc who was grinning from ear-to-ear with an I-told-you-so look on his face.

CHAPTER 15

*D*inner and the required family bonding afterwards had taken much longer than Dane liked. At the same time, he felt it had given him the time to process the clump of emotions that now sat like a log in the center of his chest.

Now, he and Zera were walking through the gardens, hand-in-hand. Never before had Dane enjoyed touching someone so much. But it seemed as if he could not keep his hands off of her. He could not resist, even the slightest touch such as earlier today when he'd tucked the wayward strands of her hair back behind her ears, or when the family had once again congregated in the living room and she'd sat at the piano beside Tamala as she demonstrated what she'd learned in her music class. Dane came up behind her, resting his hand on her shoulder, before Roark had called him away.

"Cade's back in the States but he's going to keep in touch," Roark had said when they'd walked through the French doors in the living room.

Those doors carried them out to a terrace with a stone

railing and huge potted plants. The view was breathtaking even as the sun had already set. The Donovan property was expansive. Their two hundred acres included, the XVI century house, French and English gardens, a park, swimming pool, croquet, badminton, and billiards, a farm with poultry, horses, a vegetable garden, and fruit trees. It was a French oasis located just thirty to sixty minutes away from charming medieval castles and famous vineyards.

"They're following up on everything that was in that book Zera gave to them," Roark continued. "So it should be over soon."

Dane didn't feel as optimistic as his cousin, even though he was careful not to let Zera see that.

"Have you thought about what's going to happen once this is over?" Roark asked.

"You mean if Zera will try to return to the FBI?" Dane asked and then shrugged. "I don't know how her leave of absence that turned into an extended unpaid leave works. Is she technically fired and can never go back? Or if she needs to go through the selection and training process all over again. I'm just not sure."

Roark leaned against one of the waist-high stone pillars at the edge of the terrace.

"I meant if you were going to stay here with Zera, or if the two of you are taking this "thing" you've got going back to the States?"

Dane stood with his legs partially apart facing the stretch of grass. It ran far and then dipped down a small embankment. Across from that embankment was the lake where earlier today he'd looked out the window to see two white swans gliding along as if they hadn't a care in the world. He'd envied the swans in that moment.

"I hadn't thought about what Zera and I would do once this was over," he told Roark. "There was always an agreement between us that this was just an affair."

"It's beyond that now," Roark said.

Dane shook his head. "I don't do anything beyond an affair."

Roark sighed. "I hear that and I can't say that I blame you. Too much red tape to cut through before finding success. That's the way I see it," Roark said. "But what you're saying now and what I keep seeing when the two of you are together, is a blatant contradiction. She's staying at your family's country home, meeting and mingling with members of your family. I'd say you're cruising straight toward a permanent serious relationship and waving at that affair in the rearview mirror."

Dane didn't speak immediately because for the third time tonight, one of his family members was saying something that resonated so clearly with him Dane thought they might actually be reading his mind.

"It's a difficult situation," he said. "Difficult situations tend to lead to hurt feelings and worse."

Dane stopped before saying anymore.

"You are no doubt thinking about your mother and the fact that Uncle Henry hurt her feelings so deeply all that other mess followed," Roark said.

Dane looked over to him because that's exactly what he'd been thinking.

"I don't like to think about that anymore," he admitted. "But her blood is also in me."

"You're a Donovan," Roark said. "My father used to tell me

that Donovan men love hard and fiercely. We protect and cherish what's ours. Perhaps you should think of more of that blood being in you, than the other."

Suri and the girls had come out of the house at that point, chatting about a game of billiards. Suri wanted Roark on her team. Torian and Tamala said they were drafting their father. Soon a battle was planned and Dane had watched with a touch of hope in him that he'd never thought he would experience. He'd declined a spot on either team and had suggested the walk to Zera.

Now, they walked down the steps leading out of the garden and headed towards the lake. He'd told the Interpol agents they were safe in the gardens and going toward the river because he figured they were in clear view of the house and farther back from the road. Agents were at the front gates so no one was driving through without being stopped first.

"What do you want to do when this is over?" he asked her.

"I don't know," was her immediate reply. "I guess it depends on how everything turns out."

Dane didn't want to say the words because he didn't want her to think he didn't believe in saving Hiari and the other girls.

"Over the years I've thought "what if she's dead?" more times than I can count," she continued. "But something deep down in my soul says she's not. That's why I press on."

"I've never believed anything so wholeheartedly," he told her.

"That is a shame," she said.

"Why is it a shame? Because I've never wanted to save anyone? Because I did. I wanted to save Jaydon but I couldn't."

He still felt a tinge of guilt whenever he thought about how many times he'd tried to remove Jaydon from the situation their mother had created with the Donovans. But it had already been too late, Jaydon was in until the end.

"I meant it was a shame because if you'd never believed in someone or something wholeheartedly that likely meant because you'd never invested enough of yourself in that person or that situation," she told him. "And it would be a shame to hold all that you have inside to yourself."

They walked in silence for a few more moments.

"What if I thought I might be ready to share what I hold inside?" he asked without looking at her.

"I would tell you that I was proud of you and that I wished you all the happiness in the world," she said.

Dane stopped beside a copse of trees, just a few feet away from the lake's edge. He turned her to face him, taking her other hand in his so that now he held them both.

"The only happiness I've ever experienced came from being with you," he said.

The evening was quiet, the air warm and filled with the scent of summer nights. Dane was happy in this moment because he was touching her and standing here with her. It made sense that for him, Zera was his happiness.

"That was very sweet of you to say, Dane," she replied after a moment's hesitation.

"I only say what's true, Zera. I can assure you I am not the type of man who says what I think a woman wants to hear for any reason."

"I know you're not that type of man. I also know that admitting that was not easy for you," she said. "I'm proud to be the one to have brought you happiness. And not so proud about how we've come to this point."

"It's what was supposed to be," he said and had to smile at

where he'd gotten those words. "Aunt Birdie just told us that didn't she?"

Zera grinned. "Yes she did. Aunt Birdie is a mess."

"That she is," Dane agreed.

"But she may just be one of the smartest women I've ever met," Zera continued. "She decided what she wanted for her life a long time ago and she never apologized for it or let anyone deter her. Can you imagine living with that type of brutal honesty? How many situations could be made easier if everyone were straightforward with each other?"

"Or how many people would end up in fights because of that brutal honesty?" He countered.

"Yeah," she said. "But I like her."

"Even though she's not going to die until you have my children."

Zera laughed.

Dane loved hearing that sound. He'd heard it so much tonight as Zera had interacted with the twins and when Suri amused the family with her impersonations. Dane always wanted to hear Zera laughing and to see her smiling. He wanted her to be happy.

"When this is over we're going to have a real conversation about what this affair has turned into," he said.

She stepped closer to him. "But not tonight," she whispered and slipped her hands from his to twine her arms around his neck. "Let's just be happy together tonight."

"Yeah. Let's do that," Dane said and leaned in to touch his lips to hers.

Their tongues moved slowly together in a dance that was familiar and yet, this time, different. He wrapped his arms around her waist to hold her close. Her palms moved over the back of his head sending tendrils of hunger down his spine. The kiss turned hungrier in seconds and before Dane could think better of it, he was lowering Zera to the soft grass they'd been standing on.

He lay on top of her, deepening the kiss.

One of her hands came to rest on his cheek as she pulled back slightly and nipped at his lips.

"I never stopped thinking about you, Dane. Not in all this time. You've always been in my mind," she whispered.

Dane moaned as his pulse quickened. He needed to feel her. His hands went lower and he hiked her dress up around her waist. Dane rubbed his fingers up and down her skin, loving the feel of it along her thighs and on the curve of her ass.

"I thought of you," he admitted. "I tried not to, but I couldn't stop. I needed you and I just didn't know it."

Zera lifted one leg, wrapping it around his waist while Dane kissed along the line of her jaw and down her neck.

"Dane," she whispered.

"Zera," he replied on a ragged moan.

In the next instant he was undoing his pants and when she whispered his name again, Dane ripped the thin wisp of silk away from her juncture. He wrapped her legs around his waist and sank deep into her moist core without another word.

She lifted her hips to meet his thrust and their gazes held. He was deep inside of her, so deep he thought he could touch that part of her that he never thought he wanted. It was in her eyes. The way she looked at him and the way she reached up to touch his face. Did he finally have her heart?

"Dane," she said his name again and Dane began to move inside of her.

She said it many times while he made slow love to her and

he found himself simply whispering hers as well. This was not the type of sex talk Dane was used to. Not with Zera or anyone else for that matter. But it was right. For this moment it was just him and her. Dane and Zera. Nothing more and nothing less. So when they both climaxed at the same time, it was like fate, and an earthquake. Shaking up everything in it its wake to make what was supposed to be, a reality.

"Zera," Dane whispered as he buried his face in her neck.

Their hearts beat wildly in a matching rhythm. Together, he thought. Dane wanted them to be together. Forever.

Zera felt like Cinderella awaking the night after going to the ball and meeting her Prince Charming.

No, Dane was not a prince and she had never believed in fairy tales or waiting for some man to come and rescue her from her life. But she could imagine the depth of the magic that Cinderella had experienced that night. She could imagine it because that's how Zera had felt last night being with Dane's family and then making love with him by the lake.

It had been perfect. If she were telling a story of how to be properly romanced by a man, last night would have been it.

She didn't require candlelight or flowers, love songs or gifts. Being with Dane in the company of his family, in an environment without stress or worry, was like a dream. One she had not allowed herself in the last four years.

This morning she woke to an empty room. Dane had left a note on the bed, written in his small, but neat, handwriting. Aunt Birdie requested a meeting with him, Roark, Ridge and Suri to discuss the new company. Linc and Jade were taking the girls into town to visit some of the castles in the area and Aunt Maxine was meeting with the house staff to discuss the menus for the remaining time that the family would be there. That meant Zera was on her own. Dane suggested she go for a swim and told her he would join her as soon as finished.

Zera opted to go for a walk instead. She was glad she had this time alone because she had so much to think about.

First and foremost was Dane.

So after she'd showered and dressed in white capri pants, a black tank top and her favorite polka dot tennis shoes. Zera slipped her cell phone in her back pocket and eased her sunglasses onto her face, before heading to the back of the house. She'd learned yesterday that going the back way would lead to a path that wrapped around the property. One of the Interpol agents assigned to stay at the house with them was coming in the door. His name was Jesse and he looked a lot like Chance the Rapper, which to Zera meant he seemed a bit young to be doing this job.

"Good morning, Ms. Kennedy," Jesse said as he stepped into the sunroom.

The kitchen was beside the sunroom but Zera figured that's where Aunt Maxine was meeting with the staff and she hadn't wanted to interrupt them.

"Good morning, Jesse," she replied. "I'm just going to walk around the grounds."

"Sure," he said. "It's a beautiful morning. I'll follow you. Do we need to wait for Mr. Donovan?"

"No. He's in a meeting. So it's just me," she told him.

Jesse nodded and held the door open for her.

Zera didn't mind that she wasn't totally alone. Jesse stayed a few feet back while she called Ines to check on her. They were in the States now staying at a temporary location until their permanent placement was finalized between the Marshals and the FBI.

"I love it here," she told Ines on the phone. "It's so beautiful and so quiet. So far away from everything."

"Then stay," Ines said simply.

"I can't stay here, Ines. This is the Donovan property. Am I supposed to ask them if I can rent a room?"

"No. But you're seeing a Donovan, shouldn't that give you some type of privilege to stay there after the family leaves?" Ines asked.

She was always optimistic. Always believing the best about everyone and every situation. Hiari was like that too and Zera wondered if that similarity had been one of the things that drew her to Ines.

"I don't think it works that way," Zera said and chuckled. "Besides, Dane and I—"

"Please do not say that nothing is going on between the two of you because that would just be a lie. You talk about him every time you and I speak now. I can hear it in your voice how much you like him," Ines told her.

Zera shook her head. "No. I'm not going to lie. I like him a lot."

Nobody needed to know that she was in love with Dane. That was her secret.

"Then there is no problem. Keep liking him and keep staying at that beautiful house. It's probably safe for you there anyway," she said.

"Yes, it is safer for the moment." At those words Zera turned to see that Jesse was still behind her.

He'd put on sunglasses as well. Coupled with his black suit

and shoes he looked like he could be a star in the next *Men In Black* movie. Zera smiled and turned back to the path. She was getting close to the gardens where nine-foot bushes were neatly trimmed and looked like they stood guard of the English garden with pride and victory.

"Or do you want to go back to your home in Kenya?" Ines was now asking.

"I cannot go back without Hiari," Zera replied. "My mother and my grandmother are counting on me."

"Did they say you could not come back without her?"

"No," she said.

"Oh, because I was going to say that was very foolish of them," Ines quipped. "You are not responsible for her kidnapping so you cannot be responsible for bringing her home. That is just nonsense."

"I would feel like I failed them," Zera said.

"Again with the nonsense. I am certain your family will not feel that way," Ines said.

"Well, that's how I feel—" Zera's words were paused as she thought she heard something fall.

She stopped walking and once again looked back for Jesse, but this time, he was gone.

"Shit!" Zera shouted.

"What?" Ines asked.

Zera didn't answer because she was looking around now. She didn't see anything or anyone. Something was very wrong.

"Zera? What's happening?" Ines was screaming into the phone now.

"I gotta hang up now, Ines. I'll call you back," Zera said and cut off the call.

She immediately opened her text messages and started to

type a text to Dane, but before she could finish it and hit send, her fingers froze, her heart almost stopping at the sight before her.

"Hello, Zera."

"Emmet?"

PART III

Ashes fly back into the face of him who throws them.
—*African Proverb (Nigerian)*

CHAPTER 16

"You always did follow instructions well," Emmet said when Zera stepped through the old wooden doorway.

This place looked like a shack, an old forgotten shack that could fall to the ground at any moment. Zera didn't speak, but walked all the way inside until she stood in the center of an open space. The only light came from the sun filtering in through scratched and dingy windows.

"You're not dead," she said, the words bitter in her mouth.

"And you're a liar," Emmet replied.

He closed the door, dropping a steel bar over it so that it could not be opened from the outside. The gun that he'd held to her back to get her to walk through a thick brush of trees to get here, was comfortably in his right hand.

"So now that we've gotten the pleasantries out of the way," Emmet continued. "Let's talk about the real reason I'm here."

"Because you're a sick demented criminal," she snapped.

He stepped close to her and raised his hand to slap her, but

Zera was faster. She leaned back as far as she could without falling, so his strike missed her. Emmet laughed.

"You would have learned that in your F.B.I. training," he said in a way that enunciated and separated each letter.

But that wasn't what caught Zera's attention. It was his accent.

"Who are you?" she asked and took a step back.

He looked the same as he had six months ago. He had a honey brown complexion, with dark curly hair that he wore cut low. His beard was still trimmed to a thin line along his jaw and his brown eyes still bore into her as if he had x-ray vision. Zera had always been afraid that at any moment Emmet would be able to look through her and see the truth, that she was hunting him and everyone he worked with in order to bring her cousin and the other South African girls they'd kidnapped home.

"You should have asked Aasir who I was," Emmet said.

"No," Zera gasped.

"Yes," Emmet said coming close enough so that he could reach out and rub the gun's nozzle over her temple.

Her heart sank with the thought. Emmet was African, his accent was—he'd never spoken with an accent before. Then again, neither had she, not around him anyway. They'd both hidden their true identity.

"You see, I always wondered how it was that the news of the kidnapping of that last group in Nairobi had spread so quickly. We had pulled off many in the region that were still not noted. Perhaps because the people in those villages knew what was at stake. They did not speak of it for fear we would return. It took me a while to put it together but Debare was helpful in that regard. Did you ever wonder how Aasir knew it was Debare who had taken that last group? How did he know what girls had been taken before there was any news of it in the world? Did your mother or grandmother ever tell you how they found out Hiari was gone?"

Zera felt sick. Wave after wave of horrific pain gripped her stomach and her arms instinctively went around her waist in an effort to stop them. Emmet's eyes were glazed with lunacy. She'd seen it before in videos of criminals who were being interrogated by agents, or interviews that had been conducted in jails and mental institutions. The first tendril of fear slipped down her spine.

"Who are you?" she asked again, because she had to know.

No matter what happened to her from this point on, Zera was determined to know the whole truth, once and for all.

"I am Emerho Pepple," he said. He watched her then as if waiting for her to say or do something.

Zera did neither. She simply stared at him. Emerho Pepple was Aasir's half-brother. They shared the same father, different mothers. And because Emerho's mother was jealous of Aasir's, she moved to Cameroon when Emerho was five years old. Zera only knew about him through stories that Aasir had told her. She'd never met Emerho or his mother before. And as far as she knew, Aasir had never seen his half-brother again.

"Yes, you recall now. I know Aasir told you because that is what he does. He talks and talks and talks. That is why he could not be recruited. We knew he did not have the courage to become kings the way we did. Debare had tried hard to bring Aasir on board, but he was determined to stay where he was and to work for the SSA believing in a government that was never meant to protect us or our way of living."

Tears welled in her eyes and Zera looked away from Emmet. She did not want him to see any fear or weakness, but she could not continue to look at him. Not when she was feeling the brutal sting of betrayal before he could even finish the story.

The feel of his cool lips against her cheeks had bile forming in her throat.

"Shhh, my Black Queen. Do not shed a tear for the unworthy," he whispered.

He always called her his Black Queen and Zera hated it. She hated that he'd thought she was anything to him.

"Aasir told me that Hiari had been taken. Then he called me back and said that he thought Debare was responsible," she said when she thought she could speak without vomiting. "Why?"

Zera lifted her head and stared directly into Emmet's eyes as she asked that question. "Why did all of this happen? What did I ever do to him?"

Emmet laughed. "I will tell you, because none of it matters now. You will not be able to do anything with the information that I give to you."

That meant he planned to kill her. Zera wasn't ready to die, but she would deal with that when the time came. For now, she steeled herself against all other thoughts and stared at Emmet. "Tell me," she said through clenched teeth.

He shrugged and this time rubbed the nozzle of the gun over her lips.

"Such a pretty mouth," he said, shaking his head. "A great body, lovely face, educated. That is the power of the Black Queen. I did not know this until the days before my fake death, but Aasir was in love with you. He told me he had been in love with you all of his life. You were the reason he would not turn to us. But you would not come home to him. No matter how hard he tried to convince you that your place was there in Nairobi by his side. You were to be his Black Queen."

Emmet threw back his head and laughed and Zera pushed the gun away from her face. He planned to kill her anyway, she didn't have to make it easy. Besides, he was getting off on telling her this story. Of watching her react to every malicious, but suspiciously true word that he said. She felt ill and angry and wanted to lash out. To find a gun and kill. But she'd been trained better than that. Impulsivity could lead to an agent's death, or the death of one of their teammates. Or worse, an innocent bystander. So Zera remained as calm as she could.

"He was never more to me than a friend," she replied to Emmet.

He stopped laughed instantly, looking at her with a serious gaze. "None of us are anything to you. Another trait of a Black Queen. Your heart is cold, your cut vicious and wounding."

Emmet came closer. Zera stepped back, until she came up against the wall. He pressed his body into hers.

"I did not know who you were until the very end," he said. "I thought you were my everything, that you understood me and wanted nothing more than to make me happy. Imagine how I felt when I found out I was in love with the same queen as my half-brother. It was hilarious and horrendous at the same time."

"I never asked you to love me," she said.

"No!" Emmet yelled. "But you tricked me. You got close to me and you made me believe. You did what no other man has ever been allowed to live to see done. But I've got you now."

He leaned in and licked down her cheek. Zera sucked in a breath. He moved to her ear and licked her lobe before biting down on it until she screamed.

Then he whispered, "Aasir told Debare to take Hiari to get back at you for breaking his heart. Then, when you still would not come to him, he told Debare to tell me who you really were."

Zera wanted to scream again. She wanted to punch Emmet in the face and kick him in the nuts. She wanted to fly home to Nairobi and slice Aasir's lying throat!

Instead she pushed Emmet back away from her and clutched her stomach once more.

Emmet was laughing again. He loved this. Zera didn't want to give it to him. She really didn't, but the pain was threatening to take over.

"Where is she?" Zera asked through the pain. "Where is Hiari?"

Emmet sobered again. Just like Dr. Jeckyll and Mr. Hyde his transformations were quick and diabolical.

"That bitch is dead, just like you're gonna be!" he yelled and raised his arm to point the gun at Zera's head.

Dane slammed Nyle, the Interpol agent who had driven them to Le Boulay, against the wall. His hand was wrapped in the guy's shirt and he was pressing upward so that his fist leaned hard into his throat.

Behind him Dane heard the clicking of a gun.

"Let him go, Mr. Donovan," Jon, the other Interpol agent ordered him.

"Dane," Roark said when Dane hadn't flinched nor released Nyle. "This is not helping. Let him go so they can work on finding her."

"They fucking shouldn't have lost her," was Dane's heated retort.

But a few seconds later he did release Nyle and took a step back. The agent attempted to punch Dane at that point, but Roark stepped in, grabbing the agent's wrist and shaking his head. "Not a good idea," Roark said before pushing Nyle back.

"It's not a good idea for you both to catch charges for assaulting international agents," Jon told them.

"Fuck international agents!" Dane yelled. "You can't even keep one witness safe! You can't find thousands of girls that have been taken from their homes and you can't stop one crime family from wreaking havoc across the damn globe! So yeah, fuck international agents!"

"Your language is deplorable," Aunt Birdie said as she strolled into the living room. "You are definitely Bernard's son."

Dane turned away from her. The very last thing he needed to deal with right now was Aunt Birdie.

He'd been in the meeting with her when he received the text message from an unknown number about fifty minutes ago. He'd started to delete the message, but had seen Zera's name just before he could hit the button. Once he'd opened the message Dane's entire world went dark.

I GOT YOUR LITTLE BITCH, DANE. HAVEN'T YOU EVER HEARD THE AMERICAN SAYING "BROS BEFORE HOES"? GUESS NOT SINCE YOU WERE FUCKING ZERA THE SAME TIME AS I WAS. BUT THAT'S OKAY. I'M JUST GOING TO DO HER ONE LAST TIME AND BECAUSE I KNOW THE TYPE OF MAN YOU ARE, I'LL HELP YOU OUT. YOU CAN FIND US AT THE OLD HOUSE IN THE TREES. THE DUMBASS GUARDS YOU'VE GOT DIDN'T EVEN KNOW I ARRIVED HERE AT THE SAME TIME YOU DID. SO COME ON OUT, DANE AND JOIN THE PARTY. IT'LL BE JUST LIKE OLD TIMES. I MIGHT EVEN LET YOU TAKE A TURN, BEFORE I KILL YOU BOTH!

"Emmet Parks has her," Dane said as he'd stood from the table.

Nyle was in the next room and when Dane had come out to tell him Nyle had insisted on contacting Jesse first, instead of going directly out to get Zera. Dane's rage still simmered hot and raw.

"If he hurts her," Dane told them now as the agents were still standing in the living room looking like he was speaking a foreign language.

"Hush!" Aunt Birdie said. "No need to add threatening federal agents to your assault charge."

"Thank you, ma'am," Jon said.

Aunt Birdie waved her hand in his direction. "Don't thank me," she said. "If you don't get your ass out there and bring her back here safely I'll have your badge and then I'll let him rip your balls off since it's clear you need a new pair. How the hell do you let a deranged maniac stay in a house on the property of the people you're trying to protect?"

Jon frowned and Nyle glowered. It was fine because Dane was fuming.

"I'm going to get her. You can either follow me, or sit here and twiddle your thumbs. At this point, I could care less," Dane said.

He ran up the steps and into the room where he and Zera had been staying. He went to his suitcase and retrieved the gun he'd purchased the day he'd found out Zera was an FBI agent who was working on something involving the Russian mafia. Gun in hand, Dane came back down the steps only to run into Roark.

"What are you going to do?" Roark asked.

"I'm going to shoot that sonofabitch really dead this time around," Dane told him.

Roark gave a curt nod and lifted his hand to show Dane that he had a gun too. "Let's get to it then," Roark told his cousin. "Like my daddy used to tell me, we protect our own."

They went out the front door just as two SUVs filled with more agents pulled up. Jon and Nyle were already behind Dane and Roark and they signaled for some of the other agents to head into the house and some to follow them.

Roark knew the way to the house in the trees because he and his siblings used to play out there when they were children. They arrived at the house in less than five minutes, and were just about ten miles away when they heard the first gunshot.

Dane ran harder than he ever had before, fueled by adrenaline and the pounding of his heart that he knew for certain would break into a million pieces if Zera was gone. Nothing he had—the money, cars, businesses, clothes, stocks—none of it mattered without her.

Dane saw nothing else but the house and heard nothing but the way Zera had sounded last night when she was laughing with his nieces. He ran to the door, ramming into it with his shoulder, only to be bounced back as pain soared through his body. But Dane ignored that pain. He raised his arm and shot out the windows on the side of door, going through it without a care or regard for the others who were with him.

"Welcome to the party," Emmet yelled when Dane's feet hit the floor.

He had an arm around Zera's neck and her back pulled up to his front as he used her as shield. Her face was streaked with tears but there was no blood that Dane could see.

"Ohhhhhh, look how revved up he is, Zera," Emmet said. "I knew when I heard them coming that firing a warning shot would get to him."

He chuckled, the grin spreading eerily over his face. Dane raised his gun once more. The door came crashing down seconds later and Roark and the agents poured inside. There were shouts for Emmet to drop the gun and let Zera go, at least a dozen guns were pointed at him. And at Zera.

Dane's hand shook and when she looked up at him, his heart broke with the sadness he saw in her eyes.

"Kill him," she whispered. And then in a louder voice, "Kill this evil sonofabitch!"

"Now that's not nice," Emmet said and squeezed her neck tighter. "Dane, I wanted it to just be the three of us. I told you I was gonna let you have a turn."

"You're not gonna have her," Dane told him.

His entire body trembled as flashbacks from the night he'd held a gun on his mother came roaring back to his mind. He hadn't fired the shot that night because Devlin had done it for him.

"I don't care what you've done or how you think this is gonna end, you are not going to have her."

"She's old news anyway," Emmet told Dane. "You know how much free pussy I get? Those girls have no choice but to give me whatever I want. Besides, I have to test the merchandise before I can sell it."

"Drop the gun and let the woman go!" Jon yelled. "We can take you in willingly or in a body bag. It's your choice, Parks."

"My name's not Parks!" Emmet yelled. "It's Pepple and I don't answer to you or your western laws! I was born to be a king. And she was going to be my queen."

He turned his head and kissed Zera's hair.

"I only needed to finish one more deal, but Luka wanted more girls. He wanted more merchandise to sell. I was tired of giving him my people. I'd done enough to get what I needed to be a good king. I had land, houses, cars, everything my queen would need to be happy. And then I found out she was a liar. And Luka's dumbass goons tried to kill me. But I fooled them. I fooled them all because I'm smarter," Emmet insisted. "And I'm better than you, Dane! I could have given her more than you! You are not one of us!"

"And neither are you!" Zera spat. "We would never turn against our own. You were angry that Aasir wouldn't join you. Well, I am glad he didn't because you are the coward!"

After she spoke those words, Zera elbowed Emmet hard in the abdomen. He stumbled back and his arm loosened enough at her neck for her to slip away. But Emmet was fast, he aimed the gun at Zera and opened his mouth to yell something in a language Dane did not understand.

But it didn't matter what he'd said, Dane pulled the trigger. Not once, but repeatedly as he watched Emmet's body jerk with the entry of each bullet.

Dane heard Roark saying something as he continued to pull the trigger. The gun was only making a clicking sound at this point and Emmet's body had fallen in a heap on the floor. Dane pulled away from the hand on his arm and dropped the gun to the floor. He ran to Zera just as she stood up straight and leapt into his arms. She cried, her body convulsing with the action and held onto him tightly. Dane lifted her in his arms and carried her out of the house. He carried her all the way back to the chateau and straight up to their room. She did not stop crying.

CHAPTER 17

*I*t was close to six in the evening when Dane was finally able to convince Zera to take a hot bath. Aunt Maxine had food waiting for her while Aunt Birdie waited very impatiently to see her. Dane had been adamant that everyone leave them alone once they'd returned to the house. He had no idea what Emmet had said or done to her and he did not want her upset any more than she already was.

"Just nod your head if he touched you, baby," Dane had said as he'd sat in one of the chairs in the bedroom, holding Zera on his lap.

She'd kept her face buried in his chest where his shirt was now damp from all her tears.

"Not like that," she'd finally whispered. "I told you he never touched me like that. Even though I know that's what he wanted you to think."

Dane had sent up a silent prayer.

"I'm going to run you a hot bath and then I think you need to eat something," he'd said.

"I don't want to see anyone."

Her voice seemed so small and so distant.

"No. I'll go down and get the food and bring it up to you. Nobody will come in," he promised her.

"Alright," she said and moved off his lap.

While he was in the bathroom running the water, Dane checked his cell phone. Agent LeAmbette and Cade had both sent him several text messages. He answered them now, telling them that Zera was okay but that he did not know how or why Emmet Parks had faked his death and then came back for Zera. But he was going to find out. Dane was determined to ask the questions and get the important answers with Zera this time around.

When he returned to the bedroom he saw that she was already undressing, tossing the clothes into the nearest trash can. Her polka dot tennis shoes too.

She walked naked to where he stood in the doorway of the bathroom and grabbed his hand.

"Join me," she said softly.

Dane removed his clothes and seconds later joined Zera in the soaker tub. He'd added bubbles and wasn't sure he was going to like smelling like jasmine for the rest of the night. But whatever Zera wanted, he was willing to do. He settled in behind her and leaned back against the lip of the tub. He wrapped his arms around Zera's waist and pulled her back against him. Bubbles floated around them as they sat in the hot water for endless minutes in total silence.

"How do I tell them she's gone?" Zera asked quietly.

Dane didn't think she really wanted a response, so he remained silent.

"She would be eighteen now. Her birthday was April 4th,"

she continued. "I told them, each time I spoke to them on the phone that I was going to bring her home. They thanked me for all the hard work I was doing to find her and said they couldn't wait to see us both. There was pain in their voices each time, but there was also pride. I wanted to make the pain go away for them. And for me."

She took a deep breath and Dane hugged her against him a little tighter. Zera told him everything that Emmet had said in that house, all of his sordid reasons for doing the illegal and unconscionable things he'd done. She told him about the man she'd thought was her friend, Aasir N'Joru. How he'd betrayed her.

"I know it's not my fault," she said a few moments after that recitation. "I did not order her kidnapping, just as I did not shoot Ines. But I cannot ignore that I am a common factor in what happened to both of them."

Dane could not hold his tongue any longer because he definitely did not like where he thought this conversation was going. "And so were the criminals that did what they did to both of them, Zera. You are not to blame for being the caring and intelligent person that you are. Everyone is responsible for their own actions. They are adults and they will all be held accountable."

Except for Emmet who was now, thankfully, most assuredly dead.

"He faked his death just to come back and get me. He hated me that much," she said.

"He hated himself, Zera. Emmet Parks hated everything he thought he should be, and everything he was not. He would have never been happy no matter how much money he obtained or which woman he would have ended up with," Dane told her.

"I know what you're saying is right, but it hurts Dane. It hurts so bad."

Dane kissed the top of her head. "I know it does, baby. But it's okay. I want you to let go and just hold on to me right now. I'm here for you and I'm not going anywhere."

She cried some more, turning in the tub until she could lay on his chest.

"I've got you, baby," he whispered over and over again, until she settled down once more.

～

Two days later, Zera still had a headache.

She and Dane were still at the country house along with Aunt Birdie who had been hovering and fusing over Zera every chance she could get. The other Donovans had returned to their homes. Dane laughed when Zera admitted that she liked the mean and feisty Aunt Birdie better than the concerned and not-quite-compassionate one.

Today was the day that Zera was going to speak to Necole and Cade. They were both coming to the country house to see her because Dane didn't think she was ready to return to the city just yet. He was right. She wasn't ready to go back to Paris. Zera didn't know if she ever would be.

She'd dressed in jeans and a baggy gray t-shirt, with black flats on her feet. The minute she'd come down the stairs she'd heard voices coming from the living room. She took a deep breath and released it slowly, resigning herself to whatever she was about to hear. Hiari was dead. Things could not be any worse.

They stopped talking the moment she entered the room.

Dane came over to take her hand. He led her to the couch and waited until she was seated to sit down beside her.

"How are you feeling?" Necole asked first.

She wore a skirt suit this time, navy blue with a crisp white blouse. Her hair was pulled back into a ponytail and she sat in one of the high-back Victorian chairs with one leg crossed over the other.

"I'm fine," Zera lied. Fine was something she wasn't quite sure she would feel again. "We can begin now. I'd rather get this over with."

"We understand," Cade said. "And we appreciate you typing your statement and emailing it to us ahead of time."

"No problem," Zera told them. She'd wanted to document her words for a concise record and so she would never forget all that two of her people had done to her and her family.

"So this meeting was really just a formality and a way for us to see you to make sure you were doing alright," Cade continued. "You did good, Zera. You really did."

Dane was holding her hand. He squeezed it at that moment and when she looked at him he was nodding his agreement with Cade.

"He's right. Everything you were able to find out while you were with Emmet and the book you gave us is making a huge difference. We've been able to trace some of the girls in those groups. Some of them were sold to wealthy rulers in other countries and others were sent to work in the clubs owned by the Belyakov *bratva*. But we're working with all of the countries in our agency to bring each of them home," Necole said.

"We've also been able to use some of the information you gathered to help with the investigation into the *bratva's* dealings in the States. While we still haven't arrested any of the top two operatives in the *bratva*, we're steadily chipping away at their empire. I'd say that means the four years you spent here in Paris have proven to be time well spent," Cade added.

Tears filled Zera's eyes and she didn't even care when they slid down her cheeks. Hiari would not be coming home, but her work had made a difference.

"That's wonderful news," she said anyway. "Thank you so much for keeping your word."

"The SSA also detained Aasir," Cade added. "He told them everything that he had done. He told them he knew that Emmet was still alive and that he suspected the Belyakovs had killed Debare because he was unable to bring Zera to them. He seemed to know a lot more about the dealings of the *bratva* in South Africa as well as members of actual FTOs working throughout the area. He will tell them everything, but he will never be released from prison."

Zera's hands shook as she wiped the tears from her face. Necole stood and brought a tissue box to Zera. She waited while Zera took a few and then touched a hand to Zera's shoulder.

"Cade and I have also discussed how we might be able to help you get your job back," she said.

Zera immediately shook her head. "Not yet. I'm not ready to think about any of that yet."

"Fine," Necole told her. "You let us know when you're ready."

Zera nodded and wiped her face again.

"Mr. Donovan," Carlisle said as he silently entered the room.

Dane and Cade looked at him. Carlisle stared at Dane and said, "Your guests have arrived, sir."

"Perfect timing," Dane said.

"Guests?" Zera asked when he stood.

"Just sit tight," he told her. "I'll be back in a second."

Necole stayed next to Zera while Dane was gone from the room. She rubbed her shoulder, but did not say another word. Zera was grateful because she was already tired of talking about this situation.

"My girl."

Zera's head shot up at the two words spoken in a voice that sounded just like hers. She jumped up from the couch, blinking away more tears as she ran across the room and into the arms of Jacinta Kennedy.

"My girl. My precious girl," Jacinta continued to mumble. "I have missed you so."

Zera held onto her mother until she thought she might be squeezing the breath out of her. When she finally released her the words tumbled from her lips, "Hiari is dead, mama."

Tears had already been rolling down Jacinta's deep-brown complected cheeks. "It is well," Jacinta said. "We are at peace with it, my girl. We have been for some time now."

But Zera hadn't been. She didn't know if she ever would be, but right now there was another emotion besides grief filling her soul. She turned from her mother to see Dane standing a few feet away, a small smile on his lips. She walked over to him, laying a hand on his cheek.

"You did this for me," she said softly. "You brought my mother to me because you knew I was afraid to go home to her."

Dane reached up to hold her wrist. He turned his face to kiss her palm.

"I knew that you needed to hear her tell you that what happened to Hiari was not your fault and not your responsibility," he replied. "I knew that seeing her would make you happy, Zera. And that's all I ever want is for you to be happy."

She was crying again and Zera swore she must be making up for all the years that she'd refused to let a tear drop. But even seeing Dane through bleary eyes she knew what she felt and she did not hesitate to share it this time, with him and anyone else listening.

"I love you, Dane. I love you so very much," she told him.

His smile widened and he wrapped his arms around her. "Then I'm guessing this affair is officially over because I love you too, Zera. I love you and I want to spend every day of the rest of my life with you in my arms."

Six Months Later
Oloolaimutia Hills, Kenya

*D*ane never thought he'd end up here. Not physically in Africa. That was a trip he'd always planned to take. He was referring to the fact that he was getting ready to marry someone.

Three weeks after he'd returned from the extended trip to Paris, Dane sold his house in New York and permanently moved into his house in San Francisco. With Cade and Necole's recommendations and a call from the Secretary General of Interpol, Zera had been transferred to the FBI's San Francisco office where she had been promoted to a transnational organized crime program.

Today, Dane stood by the pool at the Masai Mara Sopa Lodge. He wore all white—Gucci loafers, pants and matching dashiki with intricate gold embroidery around the collar, down the front and wrapping around both wrists. He'd put on his shades as he'd walked from the cottage on the left side of the resort's public area, where all the men had been told to stay. His hands were in his front pant pockets, his legs spread slightly, gaze intent on the breathtaking glimpse of nature stretched out before him.

The resort was located on the Maasai Mara National Reserve situated in south-west Kenya which ran alongside the Serengeti National Park in Tanzania. Together these two wonders formed Africa's most diverse and spectacular eco-systems, with possibly the world's top safari big game viewing eco-system. That's what the tour guide had told them as they'd wrapped up the 2-day safari that the event planner had arranged for the bridal party and family.

Zera wanted to combine her family's Maasai heritage with her own contemporary style. So today was their traditional wedding and sometime during the next year, they would have another ceremony—a Western ceremony as her mother had called it—to legalize their marriage in the States. Initially there had been a tug-of-war over who would pay for the wedding. Dane's desire was to give her whatever she wanted, regardless of the cost. But Zera insisted on paying for as much as she could on her own. She'd apparently been saving for this day. Her mother, Jacinta, had also saved. In the end, Dane had let the women have their way. He'd also added Zera's name to his bank account so that whatever else she needed would be at her disposal without them having to discuss the matter again.

All that was important to Dane was seeing Zera's smile. Knowing that she was safe and that each night he would climb into bed beside her. There was a time, not too long ago, that Dane hadn't been sure that would happen. He was beyond grateful for this moment.

"It is beautiful here," Bernard said coming to stand beside Dane.

He clapped a hand on Dane's shoulder and Dane nodded.

"It is," Dane conceded.

"And your wife-to-be is beautiful."

Dane's head snapped in Bernard's direction. "You've seen her?"

Bernard chuckled, his broad shoulders moving with the action. He wore the same white outfit as Dane, but his dashiki had a different gold embroidered design. Dane's two groomsmen also wore the white and gold outfit. It was what had been designed for them and approved by Zera, so no one had complained.

"No. But I've already seen her, remember? She's a beautiful woman inside and out, Dane. And she loves and respects you. When you get down to it, that's what really matters."

"I love her," Dane admitted. "I didn't think I would ever be in this place emotionally. But here I am."

"Here we both are," Bernard continued. "You in love with the woman you are planning to marry. And me, glad to be standing up for you. I'd say we've both come full circle on our journey."

Dane suspected that a big part of Bernard's declaration came from the fact that Mary Lee had accompanied him here. She'd been staying in one of the cottages with Brynne and Keysa, but she was here and from what Bernard had told him previously, the two of them were spending more and more time together. So yeah, Dane guessed, Bernard had come full circle.

"It's been one hell of a journey," Dane said. He'd never thought he would have so much emotional upheaval by the time he turned forty-two. Nor could he have imagined the happiness he would find at the end of all the turmoil.

"I have just one bit of advice for you and I know you're going to be hesitant about taking it considering all that you and I have been through," Bernard said. "But I want you to always cherish her, Dane. Second only to the Lord, she is your highest priority in this life. Respect her. Protect her. Be honest with her. Love her."

Dane listened to the words. He heard the hitch in Bernard's voice as he said the last and that final barrier that had still been lingering between them shattered. He turned so that he could face the man and removed his sunglasses. Their gazes locked, father and son, and Dane nodded because at the moment the emotion welling up in him was so thick it clogged his throat.

"I thought I loved Jocelyn," Bernard continued. "In the end I don't think I did. Not enough anyway. And your mother—" He sighed. "That was an unfortunate situation. One that you should have never had to suffer for, Son. I should have done better by you and Jocelyn, and even Mary Lee. But I didn't. I'm not ashamed to admit that now."

"You did your best," Dane said. He wondered where those words had come from. For so long Dane had thought it best to hate whichever one of the Donovan men had actually fathered him. He'd thought it was better to hate them all. But that hatred had eventually dissipated when Dane realized it would never cause the past to be erased. Everything happened as it was supposed to, good and bad, just as Aunt Birdie said. What mattered now was this moment in time.

"I'm proud to have you standing with me today…Dad." That last word almost broke him.

Bernard's strong arms going around Dane's shoulders and

pulling him in close for a tight hug, could have physically and emotionally crushed him. Instead, they empowered him. Filling him with pride and confidence that could only radiate through the bond of black men.

"I'm proud of you, Dane. You're my son. My son," Bernard repeated as he clapped his hands over Dane's back. "My son."

Zera came to a stop at the end of the sparkling gold runner that had been stretched down the twenty-foot aisle. Brown chairs with the backs covered in red and blue shuka cloth were in straight lines, rows of six across, fifteen going down.

A few feet behind her, women whom she had grown up calling aunts, but were only related by their shared culture, sang and danced. They were dressed in colorful dresses and wearing lots of jewelry. Their songs were a celebration for the creation of a new family. The words to each song meant to encourage Zera to be active in her new home and to overcome all the troubles that might come. Zera thought she and Dane had already done enough overcoming.

Zera took a step, staring down at the tip of her new polka dot tennis shoes peeking out from beneath the white gown and matching cape she wore. The outfit was beautiful and had been specially made for her. All white jacquard fabric flowed into a three foot train that followed her as she moved, the cap stopping at her ankles. Small circles of Maasai beads lined the edge of the dress's bodice and along the edges of the cape. A larger circle of beads held the cape closed and rested at the center of her chest. Therefore she was not able to wear a traditional wedding necklace. Instead, her grandmother had made Zera a special headpiece with fine Maasai beads and two thin silver chains that draped low on her forehead.

Her mother stood to her right at Zera's request, her grandmother to her left. They were both dressed in traditional Maasai dresses, matching headpieces wrapped to sit high on their heads. As Zera had never known her father, she wanted to be presented to Dane anyway. She saw him waiting for her, his all white attire accented his rich mocha skin tone. Beside him was his father, Roark and Cade Donovan. They all looked debonair and serious. But Zera's heart only beat for Dane.

Look how far they'd come. It had taken them four years to get to this point. Four years, her kidnapped cousin, two deranged and obsessed men and a direct connection to a Russian *bratva*, to be exact. Damn, she loved this man. It had begun in those first days all those years ago, but in the last nine months that feeling had truly blossomed to the point that Zera thought it might actually overtake her.

But Dane would never allow that to happen. He loved her and because of that loved, he'd moved across the country so that she could accept a promotion to a unit that would focus on bringing down the Belyakov *bratva* and any other organizations like it that thought human trafficking was just a quick get-rich scheme. Dane had even supported her desire to have a traditional wedding ceremony first, even though it would not be a legal joining. Zera would most happily marry Dane again, and again.

Her smile was bright as she made her way down the aisle to finally lock hands with Dane.

Behind her, Ines and Dane's sisters—Brynne and Keysa— walked wearing white mermaid skirts and sleeveless gold lace applique tops. He held her hand and together they watched as the ladies came dancing down the aisle. They were joined by a group of men who made their way across the front of the altar, to join the ladies going back up the aisle. It was at that point that everyone joined in with the singing and dancing. The words and dance steps had been taught last night during the family dinner.

More members of Dane's family than Zera had imagined had come to the ceremony. Roark, Ridge, Suri and Aunt Maxine. Aunt Birdie who flat out told Zera last night that she would not be singing or dancing today, sat with her arms folded, a ghost of a smile etching her face. Henry and Beverly Donovan were sitting on the front row. Linc, Jade and the twins were beside them. To some shock, Linc and Jade had announced last night that they would be opening a new casino in Paris. Bailey Donovan and her husband Devlin were also present. As well as Albert Donovan, his son Brock and Brock's pregnant wife, Noelle.

Zera had been happy to meet them all and was actually looking forward to being part of such a big family.

The significance of this ceremony was for the community to see her and Dane together, rather than them just signing a document. For her people it was more about the union and how the new couple would interact with their community. As Zera and Dane stood at the altar they hugged and shared a quick kiss, before turning to face their guests. But just as more music and dancing were to begin, Zera spotted a familiar face in the crowd.

Necole LeAmbette was there and sitting right beside her was...Zera gasped. She clamped a hand to her chest and felt Dane wrap his arm around her to keep from falling.

"Hiari?"

Necole saw that Zera had seen her and she stood, taking the hand of the woman that had been sitting beside her. They walked down the aisle to audible gasps. Zera could hear her mother and grandmother singing.

"Emmet Parks was a liar and a criminal, Zera," Necole said. "I never stopped looking for her or any word of what had actually happened to her. We found another girl from their group and she told us that Hiari had been sold to a couple in Malaysia. I promised you I would bring her home and I did."

"Zera," Hiari said in a voice that was the best music Zera could ever hear.

She looked the same, but she had grown taller. Her hair was ruthlessly short but her brown eyes were still beautiful and her high cheekbones matched Zera's and their grandmother's.

"Hiari," Zera said and pulled her cousin into her arms.

There was nothing better, Zera thought hours later when Dane was sitting at the table beside her watching as their guests continued to dance, sing and eat until the late hours of the night. Hiari did not dance, but she had smiled as she sat near their grandmother. She smiled and she looked around the room to find Zera's gaze often.

No, Zera thought again, there was nothing better than this. Her life, her people, and her loves.

THE DONOVAN FAMILY TREE

Download the Donovan Family Tree:

http://www.acarthur.net/download/3056/

1ST GENERATION

Elias (d) & Gertrude Donovan (d) – Children: Rowan (m. Adeline) and
Charleston (m. Cora)

Rowan (d) & Adeline Donovan (d) – Children: Isaiah (m. Dorethea), Aaron [d] (m. Sondra), Abraham (never married) and Bridgette a.k.a. Birdie (never married)

Charleston (d) & Cora Donovan (d) – Children: Cephus (m. MingLee), Joanna (m. Johnathan Bowers), Katherine (d) (m. Myles Denton), Della (m. Robert Sats)

2ND GENERATION

Isaiah "Ike" (d) & Dorethea "Dot" Donovan (d) – Children: Albert (m. Darla[d]), Henry (m. Beverly), Bernard (m. Jocelyn), Everette (m. Alma), Reginald (m. Carolyn) and Bruce (m. Janean)

   Aaron [d] & Sondra – Child: Gabriel (m. Maxine)

   Abraham "Abe" Donovan – Child: Margo (m. Klevon Whitfield)

   Bridgette "Birdie" Donovan – No Children

Cephus & Ming Lee – Children: Charles (m. Brenda), Wen (m. Hugo Norton)

   Joanna & Johnathan Bowers – Children: (twins) Loretta (m. Billy Ringgold), Lorraine (m. Jerry Seavers)

   Katherine "Kay" (d) & Myles Denton (d) – Children: Myles, Jr. (m. Alice)

   Della & Robert – No Children

3RD GENERATION

Albert & Darla – Children: Brock (m. Noelle), Brandon (m. Amber) and Bailey

   Henry & Beverly – Children: Lincoln (m. Jade), Trenton (m. Tia) and Adam (m. Camille)

   Bernard & Mary Lee (x) – Child: Keysa (m. Ian)

   Bernard & Jocelyn – Child: Brynne

   Everette & Alma – Children: Maxwell (m. Deena) and Benjamin (m. Victoria)

   Reginald & Carolyn – Children: Savian (m. Jenise), Parker (x Jaydon (d)) (Adriana), and Regan (Gavin)

Bruce & Janean – Children: Dion (m. Lyra) and Sean (m. Tate)

Gabriel & Maxine – Children: Roark, Ridgely and Suri

Margo & Klevon – Children: (triplets) Alexis, Adonna and Amelia

Charles & Brenda – Children: Cadence "Cade", Dakota

Wen & Hugo – Child: Xia

Loretta & Billy – Children: Maria, Morganna & Hannah

Lorraine & Jerry – Children: Kendra & Cecile "CeeCee"

Myles Jr. & Alice – Child: Myles, III

4TH GENERATION

Brock & Noelle

Brandon & Amber – Child: Serene

Bailey & Devlin

Lincoln & Jade – Children: Torian & Tamala

Trenton & Tia – Child: Trevor

Adam & Camille – Children: Josiah, Jordan

Dane & Zera

Keysa & Ian – Child: Madison Lee

Brynne & Wade

Maxwell & Deena – Child: Sophia

Benjamin & Victoria – Child: Aria

Savian & Jenise

Parker & Adriana

Regan & Gavin – Child: Raleigh

Dion & Lyra – Child: Ilyssa

Sean & Tate – Child: Briana

******Key: m = married; [d] = deceased; x = divorced

THE DONOVAN SERIES

The Seniors are listed in order by birth and their children are listed below them (also in order by birth)

Senior — Albert Donovan

Brock & Noelle — Book 4: FULL HOUSE SEDUCTION

Brandon & Amber — Book 13: IN THE ARMS OF A DONOVAN

Bailey & Devlin — Book 14: FALLING FOR A DONOVAN

* * *

Senior - Henry & Beverly Donovan

Lincoln & Jade (Children: Twin daughters, Torian & Tamala) — Book 1: LOVE ME LIKE NO OTHER

Trenton & Tia (Child: Son, Trevor) — Book 3: DEFYING DESIRE

Adam & Camille (Children: Sons, Josiah and Jordan) — Book 2: A CINDERELLA AFFAIR

* * *

Senior – Bernard & Jocelyn Donovan

Keysa & Ian — Book 6: HOLIDAY HEARTS

Brynne & Wade — Book 15: DESTINY OF A DONOVAN

* * *

Senior – Everette & Alma Donovan

Maxwell & Deena (Child: Daughter, Sophia) — Book 5: TOUCH OF FATE

Benjamin & Victoria (Child: Daughter, Aria) — Book 9: PLEASURED BY A DONOVAN

* * *

Senior – Reginald & Carolyn Donovan

Parker & Adriana — Book 11: EMBRACED BY A DONOVAN

Savian & Jenise — Book 12: WRAPPED IN A DONOVAN

Regan & Gavin (Child: Son, Raleigh) — Book 10: HEART OF A DONOVAN

* * *

Senior - Bruce & Janean Donovan

Dion & Lyra (Child: Daughter, Ilyssa) — Book 7: DESIRE A DONOVAN

Sean & Tate (Child: Daughter, Briana) — Book 8: SURRENDER TO A DONOVAN

≈

Monica & Alexander — WINTER KISSES

Karena & Samuel (Child: Son, Elijah) — SUMMER HEAT

Deena & Maxwell (Child: Daughter, Sophia) — Book 5: TOUCH OF FATE

THE DONOVAN SERIES & THE DONOVAN FRIENDS BOOKS IN READING ORDER:

Book 1: LOVE ME LIKE NO OTHER

(Lincoln Donovan & Jade Vincent)

Book 2: A CINDERELLA AFFAIR

(Adam Donovan & Camille Davis)

Donovan Friends #1:

GUARDING HIS BODY

(Lorenzo Bennett & Sabrina Desdune)

Book 3: DEFYING DESIRE

(Trent Donovan & Tia St. Claire)

Book 4: FULL HOUSE SEDUCTION

(Brock Remington & Noelle Vincent)

Book 5: TOUCH OF FATE

(Maxwell Donovan & Deena Lakefield)

Donovan Friends #2:

SUMMER HEAT

(Samuel Desdune & Karena Lakefield)

Donovan Friends #3:

WINTER KISSES

(Alexander Bennett & Monica Lakefield)

Book 6: HOLIDAY HEARTS

(Ian Sanchez & Keysa Donovan)

Book 7: DESIRE A DONOVAN

(Dion Donovan & Lyra Anderson)

Book 8: SURRENDER TO A DONOVAN

(Sean Donovan & Tate Dennison)

Book 9: PLEASURED BY A DONOVAN

(Benjamin Donovan & Victoria Lashley)

Book 10: HEART OF A DONOVAN

(Regan Donovan & Gavin Lucas)

(Brynne Donovan & Wade Banks)

Donovan Friends #7:

FOR ALWAYS

(Tyler West & Gabriella Bennett)

ALSO BY A.C. ARTHUR

OTHER CONTEMPORARY ROMANCE

The Office Series

Book 1: OFFICE POLICY

Book 2: CORPORATE SEDUCTION

* * *

The Indecent Series

Book 1: INDECENT PROPOSAL

Book 2: INDECENT EXPOSURE

* * *

Rules of the Game Trilogy

Book 1: RULES OF THE GAME

Book 2: REVELATIONS

Book 3: REDEMPTION

* * *

The Carrington Chronicles

Book 1: WANTING YOU - Part One

Book 2: WANTING YOU - Part Two

Book 3: NEEDING YOU

Book 4: HAVING YOU

* * *

The Rumors Series

Book 1: RUMORS

Book 2: REVEALED

* * *

The Royal Weddings

Book 1: TO MARRY A PRINCE

Book 2: LOVING THE PRINCESS

Book 3: PRINCE EVER AFTER

Book 4: TAMING THE PRINCE

* * *

The Taylors of Temptation

Book 1: ONE MISTLETOE WISH

Book 2: ONE UNFORGETTABLE KISS

Book 3: ONE PERFECT MOMENT

* * *

OBJECT OF HIS DESIRE

UNCONDITIONAL

LOVE ME CAREFULLY

HEART OF THE PHOENIX

SECOND CHANCE, BABY

SING YOUR PLEASURE

DECADENT DREAMS

EVE OF PASSION

~

PARANORMAL ROMANCE

The Shadow Shifters

Book 1: TEMPTATION RISING

Book 2: SEDUCTION'S SHIFT

Book 3: PASSION'S PREY

Book 4: SHIFTER'S CLAIM

Book 5: HUNGER'S MATE

Book 6: PRIMAL HEAT

Book 7: A LION'S HEART

* * *

The Damaged Hearts Series

(Shadow Shifters Spinoff)

Book 1: MINE TO CLAIM

Book 2: PART OF ME

Book 3: HUNGER FOR YOU

Book 1-3: DAMAGED HEARTS BOX SET

* * *

The Wolf Mates

The Alpha's Woman (Available as part of the GROWL Anthology
and CLAIMED BY THE MATE VOL.1 Duology)

Her Perfect Mates (Available as part of the WILD Anthology and
CLAIMED BY THE MATE VOL.2 Duology)

Bound to the Wolf (Available as part of the HUNGER Anthology and CLAIMED BY THE MATE VOL.3 Duology)

CONTEMPORARY SMALL TOWN ROMANCE (W/A LACEY BAKER)

The Sweetland Series

Book 1: HOMECOMING

Book 2: JUST LIKE HEAVEN

Book 3: SUMMER'S MOON

YOUNG ADULT PARANORMAL (W/A ARTIST ARTHUR)

The Mystyx Series

Book 1: MANIFEST

Book 2: MYSTIFY

Book 3: MAYHEM

A Mystyx Novella: MUTINY

Book 4: MESMERIZE

ABOUT THE AUTHOR

Stay in touch with A.C. on the web!

Be the first to know when A.C. Arthur's next book is available! Follow her at BookBub to get an alert whenever she has a new release, preorder, or discount!

Visit the "Contact" page on her website, www.acarthur.net, to sign up for her monthly newsletter.

"Follow", "Friend" and/or "Like" her on Facebook (AC Arthur's Book Lounge), Twitter (@ACArthur), Pinterest (acarthur22), Instagram (@acarthurbooks), Tumblr (acarthurbooks), Google Plus and GoodReads.

$ 14.99

Made in the USA
Middletown, DE
07 July 2024

57004833R00150